Long Before Morning

Also by Cade Jay Hathaway

Happy Endings Sleepover
Sander's Courage

Long Before Morning

A Happy Endings Sleepover Novel — No. 3

By

Cade Jay Hathaway

—————————————

Long Before Morning

LIBRARY OF CONGRESS CATALOGING-IN-PUBLICATION DATA

Hathaway, Cade Jay
Long Before Morning / Cade Jay Hathaway 1991—
p. cm.
ISBN-13: 978-1522844907   ISBN-10: 1522844902
1. Contemporary Gay Life—Fiction. 2. Life in Denmark—Fiction.
3. CIA / Espionage—Fiction. 4. Contemporary Youth Relationships—Fiction. I. Title
Printed in the United States of America
Set in **Palatino Linotype** — Book Designed by Wilson Rushbrook
Final Proofreading by Gabriel Williamson

10 9 8 7 6 5 4 3 2 1   FIRST EDITION

Author's note:

Certain characters in this novel speak various European languages. Whenever a character is heard speaking English as a second language, the writing reflects whatever limitations that particular character may have with grammar, accents, or pronunciations of certain English words and phrases. However, if the character is thinking any unexpressed narrative thoughts, those thoughts will reflect the usage of proper grammar and pronunciation as if the person is thinking in his or her native language.

Acknowledgments

"...Sometimes, you can attempt to make all the difference in the world, and it still is like trying to stem the tide with a sieve. The moral of this story is that no matter how much we try, no matter how much we want it ... some stories just don't have a happy ending."

These are the words of Jodi Picoult as written in her wonderful book, *Leaving Time*. Whenever something awful happens—usually it is something that we see others experience through a television lens—we never imagine that whatever it is could ever touch our own lives. Why is that? Why *not* us? Bad things happen to good people, and good things happen to bad people. And so it goes, and always will.

Many of you who have followed my relatively short career as an author of gay fiction will know that my stories in this *Happy Endings Sleepover* series are autobiographical. My family here in Denmark say that they're closer to the truth than anyone who becomes a subject in them is sometimes comfortable with. But them's the breaks when you're living with a burgeoning writer who's still getting his sea legs.

So it figures that life will eventually catch up with wherever the Happy Endings are, and so it did for us. I assure you that I'm not revealing any spoilers. Soon you'll embark on the latest four-hundred-page adventure with the Hansen-Allen family, and what will be will be. But for now, it's time for a list of acknowledgments. These people are my heart and soul, and they have and always will be my life.

Therefore, I acknowledge . . .

Lasse Jørgensen. These next three words say it all, especially now: I Love You. **Peter Mads Jannik Jørgensen**, you are the world's Jiminy Cricket. You make us look at ourselves and take stock. I hope we pass. The **Family Jørgensen**. Words don't work, and I start to tear up whenever you cross my mind and heart. You can fill in the blanks. **Evelyn Barnes**. You are my mom, aunt, sister, and friend all rolled into one sweet, convenient package. Thanks for not flushing an errant newbie down the government commode when you had every right to do so. You did your country a disservice, and I'm mighty glad that you did! You're my favorite lezzy!

My baby brother and sister, **Benny** and **Maisey Cooper**, are two of the best people inhabiting this or any planet. I'm sorry our mom is our mom! Maybe someday she'll break out of her cultish cocoon and see the life she's missed. But until then, let's all three just love her and accept her for who she is. There's always hope! Besides, it won't be long until you're old enough to call your own shots.

And a huge thanks goes out to **D.P. & Sons Publishers** and their **Cerulean Sky Press** imprint. **Davey Porter**, whatever you saw in me and these scrawls of mine, I want you to know how much I appreciate your belief in me. I know how hard the job you have can be, and you'd have better odds in Vegas at an off-the-strip casino.

Finally, to everyone who stayed with these books past page 25, the *Happy Endings Sleepover* novels mean absolutely nothing without you. Please accept my gratitude.

With much love,

November 8, 2015
Copenhagen, Denmark

For the Light We Call Forgiveness . . .

Prologue

I T IS SO HARD TO WALK from the train

station to the taxi stand when you're dead tired and have been awake for going on twenty hours straight. But I wanted to get the hell home. I'd been away for nearly a month in Ukraine, and I had never felt so good crossing back into Denmark as I had earlier this morning.

In case we're meeting for the first time, my name is Johnnie Allen. I'm a twenty-five-year-old American who has made Denmark his home for the past five years. I'm a career field officer for the United States Central Intelligence Agency, and I am posted to Denmark as a Transportation Specialist.

In a nutshell, my job is to ferry U.S. and allied intelligence assets into and out of places that they really shouldn't be. Sometimes those places belong to American allies; most of the time they do not. It's the 'most of the time' jobs that create the pucker factor, and I admit I've had my share of days that haven't gone quite as planned. But I'm still here to talk about them, and so far I've yet to see the wrong side of the bars in a foreign jail cell.

I have a wonderful family in Denmark. There is my husband and life partner, Sander Lars Hansen. If you haven't figured out the math on that, we're gay, and happily married.

My extended family includes my beautiful mother-in-law, Magda; my awesome father-in-law, Niels; and sweet sister-in-law, Ingrid—she's a couple years older than me, and is an awesome person. Then there's my brother-in-law, Jannik, who is in his early teens. He's really like a surrogate son to me, and he self-reports that Sander is not just his brother, but is also his best friend.

Normally I would have called Sander from Copenhagen and asked him to meet me a couple hours later at the Gelsted railway station for the lift home. Sometimes he even drives the half hour into Odense and collects me there so we can have dinner out at one of our favorite eateries for a little alone time before heading home for some much needed *exercise.* I do look forward to the exercise, no matter how bushed I may be.

This trip I'm home a week earlier than I expected, so I thought I'd surprise my man by knocking on the door and watching his face when he answers. But when the cab dropped me off I could see that no one was home. Darn it! Oh, well. Just him finding me at home when he gets back from wherever he's gone will work just as well. Maybe I'll get all naked and lie face down on the bed, having strategically placed a piece of masking tape by my ass crack with the words 'Insert Here' written on it in Sharpie pen. I'll trade surprise for a good laugh any day.

I went upstairs to drop off a present in the little recording studio we'd help build for Jannik—he's quite the composer and musician. I'd found a great deal on some Bang & Olufsen speakers at, of all places, the duty free shop in the Berlin airport. So I set them by his keyboard and sat down on Jannik's daybed for just a second. But within a minute I had laid down and was immediately lost to the world in a hard, deep sleep.

It was the laughter that triggered me awake, some three or four hours later. It sounded like Pokey talking with someone on the phone. Probably Jannik.

Long Before Morning

I sneaked down the back stairs that leads to the kitchen in the hope that my little plan remained salvageable. If I could quickly slide over to the hall should his attention be elsewhere, I could still strip and be on the bed to spring my surprise.

With careful steps I rounded the corner from the dining room into the Great room, and that's when I saw them.

PART ONE

JOHNNIE PAUL ALLEN

Chapter 1

I AM SIX. I am considered a sweet boy. I am a

golden boy. A yellow-haired tow-head, with bright blue eyes, people like me immediately. I am stereotypical. I am fucking cute! These are the things my Grammy and my Aunt Jean tell me. Hell if I know what a tow-head is, but it doesn't sound very fun. My name is Johnnie Paul Allen and I love everybody, and everybody loves me.

My daddy drives a bus. The kind that goes all the way across the whole country. Sometimes he lets me ride to the first town, and my mommy picks me up there and we go to Jack-in-the-Box for a milk shake and French fries.

I get to play with so many things. Toys. Games. Friends. And of course, our dog, Stump. He's very funny sometimes, and he poops a lot. That makes grown-ups very angry. They don't like dog poop. Sometimes Stump eats it. Maybe he must think it's a Tootsie Roll. He's not the smartest dog.

My grandpa is my best friend. I call him Grampy. He's very fun to be with and he takes me places that are so much fun. He loves me, too, but big boys can't say that they love you because that's for girls, he says. But I know he does.

I like music and songs, and I sing to myself because I'm really quite good, I think. I know very many songs, but not the stupid ones—well, I *know* them, but I don't sing them. Mary can take her little lamb and eat it for Sunday supper for all I care. And, duh, I know that the wheels on the bus go round and round. What else are they gonna do?

I like real music. Like the kind that's on the radio. And my Grampy has so many records and CDs. He has both, and they need different kinds of machines to play them, but I'm an expert on how to use them. Just ask me if you need any help.

I saw a band that I like very much. They were on the T.V. on a show Grammy watches called *Live with Regis & Kathie Lee*. I like them so much. Not Regis and Kathie Lee. I like the band. They are called Hanson. They sang very good and so I looked for their CD when we went to the Fred Meyer's store. I found it. I wanted it. Badly.

"Whatcha got there, Stomper?" Grampy says. He calls me Stomper because when I first started to walk on my very own, I guess I sort of stomped across the floor. Sometimes he calls me Stomps for short. "Looks like a new record. Is it a hit?" he smiles.

"I don't know what that is, Grampy," I say. "But I really, really, really like it a lot."

"Who's it by?" he asks. I tell him it's Hanson, and that Grammy and me watched them on the T.V. and that I don't know for sure, but I think she liked them too. "Well, we better get it before somebody else does," he laughs. "Put it in the buggy."

My mom doesn't call it a buggy. She calls it a cart. But I like buggy better. I get to stand on the end of it facing backwards, and hold on as Grampy pushes me through the store. He calls me his rubber baby buggy bumper, but I'm not a baby or a bumper—and I'm not made out of rubber. But I laugh every time he says it.

The ladies in the store all smile at us when we ride by, and their kids have to sit in the stupid floppy seat up by the pushing bar. I don't. I figure if I did, and didn't want to sit there, a couple of kicks to the driver would probably get me out of there. That's

21

why my mom makes me walk alongside the cart and hold on to it.

Grampy pushes us to all of the fun parts of the store while Grammy gets the groceries. We go to the toys, and to the fishing stuff, and to the tires. Grampy always has to look at the tires because he's waiting for them to be on sale. "Never pay full price for tires, kid," he tells me. "Only boobs pay full price. And nobody ever got anything on sale at Costco, either! Their prices all look fine and dandy, but they make it all back with that damned card they make you buy every year. Seems like I just pay for it, then along comes another bill for another year. They getcha both ways, I tell ya!"

"They getcha comin' and goin'," I agree.

"If it ain't up, it's down!" he says.

"If it ain't one thing, it's another," I mimic.

"You got it figured, Stomps! Never forget it!"

We stop and check out the tents and the camping stuff. I could live in a tent very easily! I love looking at tents here because they're all set up and I can play in them while Grampy looks at the tires. At Walmart they just have these dopey little model tents to look at that maybe Barbie or G.I. Joe could sleep in. But that's all. Personally, I want to see my tent and try it out before I get it.

"Knock knock! Anybody home?" It's Grammy outside my tent. Her buggy's full of groceries, and I'm really happy because I see two boxes of Captain Crunch, and two more of Count Chocula cereal. Maybe they might go for a bowl of the Crunch, but those Choculas are for me!

"Nobody here but Johnnie. Is that my Grammy?" I ask, playfully. "What's the secret code?"

"The code is: It's a long walk home if you don't get your butt out here, pronto!" she laughs.

"I'm coming. Keep your hat on," I joke. She doesn't really wear a hat, but she told me that when she was young, everybody did. Boys and girls both. I heard her say that thing about the hat to Grampy when he's in the car hooting the horn at her.

"Where's the old guy?" she asks. "As if I didn't know."

"Tires!" I report. "He's checking if they're on sale."

"He never tires of tires," she chuckles. I've heard her say that a bajillion times, but I laugh every time she says it. You have to laugh when old people say funny things, even if they're not that funny. "Well, let's roll over there before he buys up Good Year," she says.

Long Before Morning

GRAMPY AND GRAMMY have a station wagon. Grampy calls it The Original SUV. I like it because it's so big and the whole back seat is all for me, and only me. I love to stay with them.

We've been listening to Hanson the whole way. It was fun to watch Grampy cuss at the CD because he couldn't get the plastic wrap to cooperate. Grammy finally ordered him to give it to her, and she just sliced a hole with her pen knife and gave it back to him.

"Here you go, Mister Puffenstuff!" she says, all like she's the boss that knows better.

"You cheat, woman!" he laughs. "You can't use tools!" She laughs, too, and elbows him a little. That's their lovey-dovey thing they do. Then Grampy passes the CD case back to me and I just stare. I stare at the three boys on the cover, and I wish they were my brothers. I wish they were my friends, and I wish I could be one of them. Then I hear the song I love the best: *MMMBop!* It's so awesome! I love to hear them sing so much, and the one boy, Zac, plays the drums.

I'm looking at the picture of Zac Hanson and I feel funny. I look at his butt and where his thing is.

My thing does that thing where it gets really ___, and pops out, and when the tip of it rubs against my undies it tickles. I like that feeling.

It's the middle of summer vacation. I don't miss school. Three weeks ago we had fireworks, and I got to hold sparklers for the first time. My mom was a big baby about it, and Daddy was on a bus trip to Washington D.C. He got to see the Beach Boys play their music in front of lots and lots of people. Grampy told Mom to give the kid a damned sparkler. Worse that could happen is I'd catch on fire and we'd have the best fireworks show in the neighborhood, he said. So I got to hold the sparklers!

That day is America's birthday, so I thought it would be only right that I sing the birthday song while I held my flaming sticks.

"Happy birthday to you!"

"Johnnie!!!"

"Happy birthday to you!"

"Be careful!!!"

"Happy birthday, dear America-a-a-a-a-a..."

"Oh, hell, Leann! Leave the kid alone, I swear!"

"Happy birthday to you!!! — And many more, on channel four!" There! I got it all out! And I haven't exploded into eleventy-million burning, flaming bits, either! Like Cartman says: *You can suck mah balls!* Cartman is the best.

We're almost back at Grampy and Grammy's house. They said that after supper we can drive over to The Plunge. It's a real big swimming pool and I can go as far as the big number '4' painted on the side of the pool. But not more than that.

Look! There it is! We drive by and there's a big sign that Grammy reads.

SATURDAY, JULY 26TH
"DUNK YOUR KID DAY!"
BOYS AND GIRLS 12 AND UNDER SWIM FREE!

Grammy's happy as can be because she can save money. And besides, since she will just sit on one of those long chairs that you stick your legs out with (and wear sunglasses on), the only one that has to pay is Grampy. And he's old, so he gets half price anyway! What a deal! Maybe afterwards we can get a frozen yogurt out of the deal if I make sure to say all the right stuff to Grammy. Because, according to Grampy, she's the keeper of the gold. I like this day.

JOHNNIE IS ELEVEN

I'M ELEVEN NOW, AND I HATE SCHOOL so goddamned fucking much that there are no fucking words for it. Fuck! There just aren't *words*.

Every damned day it's the same big hassle. That's all it is! And I play by the rules. I do! I get the best grades of anybody that I know of, and still it's not fucking enough! It's never enough!

I don't fit in at all, ever. Not with the teachers (well, most of them), not with the other kids, and definitely not with my mom and step-dad. You know why? Because when I'm not at Hell School, I'm in Real Hell... Church! My mom is a psycho church lady, and my shitty step-fuck is just as bad.

Why can't I ever fit in? *Just, why?!* I know the reasons, never mind.

Why don't I fit in with the other kids? Because I don't like what they like. I like smart stuff, not dumb stuff. And I like other boys. I mean, I *like* other boys. I don't like girls; in *that* way, anyways. I try my best to keep it to myself, but whenever I'm dumb enough to trust somebody with such personal information, you can guess what happens next. It's all over the school. It's all over the cafeteria at lunchtime. I'm surprised

27

they don't print it on the school menu: *Johnnie's a fag! He's into dudes, man!*

Number two: I hate church and all religions. I think it's dumb as can be, and I get in trouble all the time at Sunday School because I dare to question their dumb-ass stories (lies, really...), and boy, does that make 'em sore! You'd think I killed a baby, the way they react when I ask if the "teacher" really believes a snake conned a dumb girl into eating an apple. And so what if she did? She just wanted to use the brain "God" gave her to determine if he was full of shit or not. So for that she gets a stinky, bloody period once a month, and drags her husband down with her! And they even get evicted from their home. Sounds fair to me—not! Such a loving god (small 'g').

So it all went to shit after that, and I didn't get given the snack of Fig Newtons and grape Kool-Aid. There I go, missing out again! Oh, and I've heard whispers that I'm "one of *those*..." which can only mean one thing: that they're gossiping that I'm into boys. Maybe I should've tried the Catholics. But according to my mom, Catholics aren't Christians— they're just Catholics, and they follow a false Papist doctrine that doesn't believe in salvation.

According to the geniuses at the all-knowing First Baptist Church of Auburn, the Catholics believe they can only get to Heaven by their works. But—and this was the deal killer for me—if Hitler had asked for Jesus to come into his heart just before he poisoned Eva Braun with cyanide, and blew his brains out all over the bunker wall, he would be welcomed into everlasting glory. Oh, and those six million Jews that he stuffed into the ovens are all in Hell, by the way, because none of them would have been saved. After all, they don't believe in the whole Jesus thing, and besides, those Jews are Christ killers anyways. So says the brain trust at their church. For this I get socially crucified myself; not only at the cult—*I mean church*—but in my own house as well.

And finally, my parents... So I don't like them very much. They're way too hard on me. That's one thing. But I have a cute little sister and brother—Benny and Maisey—and they're just three years old, but our mom and their dad just yell at them all the time. It makes me sick. They're little kids! They're not little Christian robots who have to be perfect all the time. I think the fact that they're not perfect is what *makes* them perfect. But they don't see it that way.

If Benny grabs some extra cookies or spills something on the kitchen floor, they yell at him like he just personally insulted Ronald Reagan. (I don't exactly know what that means, but Grampy says it all the time about them, so according to my keepers, it must be bad to insult Ronald Raegan.)

"What the Sam Hill is your momma so upset about?! Benny's toys bein' on the floor?! You'd think he insulted Ronald Reagan, or something!" he says. "Don't she know that kids play with toys?! Makes me wish that when she was a tot, I'd have washed her damn mouth out with soap just for breathing air!" And that makes me laugh! Grampy makes things good again. Oh, and they know I like boys, too. That's another reason I don't like my mom and her husband. I should probably tell you how they know that I like boys and not girls. Especially since it almost got Grampy sent to the hangman's noose at the prison in Walla Walla.

I was sitting at the kitchen table drawing submarines and *Star Trek* spaceships one afternoon. My mom was cooking supper and I was just sitting there minding my own business. Mom's man was at work.

"Johnnie, did you guys finish your square dance thing in Ms. Billings' class yet?" she asked me. I told her that we had, and she wondered if we were gonna show the parents at the Christmas pageant before school let out for winter break. I told her that we would.

Then she asked who I danced with. I told her it's square dancing. You dance with everybody when you square dance. But she wouldn't drop it. She wanted to know who my partner was at the start and the end of the dance. So I told her. Grace Clark.

"Do you like her?" Mom asked. I told her, yeah, Grace is nice. After all, I've known her since kindergarten. "I can't place her... Is she the curly haired blond girl with the handicapped brother?"

"Yeah. His name is Marty. And yeah, that's her," I reported.

"They're Mormons, I think," she mused. With Mom, everything can be reduced down to what religion you are, and whether or not you've said the sinner's prayer. "Is she your girlfriend?"

"No. She's not my girlfriend," I mutter. This is so uncomfortable.

"Have you ever been in love yet, sweetie?"

How do I answer this? Yes, I have been—in fact I am—in love. I don't wanna lie. It's bad enough just keeping private things to myself when all I ever hear is how bad I am, and that I'm gonna be burning in Hell for-e-ver! For-fucking-e-ver! I just couldn't take it anymore.

"Yes, Momma. I've been in love," I told her.

31

"Wow! That's wonderful! Will you tell me who? This is so exciting!" she giggled, as she turned the pans off and practically skipped over to the table and sat down. It'd been a long time since I'd seen her giggly-happy, and I love it when she's like that.

"Nah! No way!" I said.

"John-John! Come on!" she laughed. "You know you can tell your ol' ma anything! I promise I'll keep it between us! I mean it!"

"Not even Bill?" I said.

"I promise. On the Bible! You have my word. I just wanna know so I can be happy for you!" she enthused with such sincerity.

"Well..."

"Come on! I'm dying to know!" she grinned. She was so much fun in that moment.

"Okay. Well, you know my friend, Cameron Daniels?" I began.

"Is it his sister, Jessica? Oh my God, she is just darling! When did you guys become boyfriend-girlfriend?" she asked.

"Well, it's not Jessica. It's... It's, uh, Cameron." There, I'd said it. It was out. My mom knew, and at least now I wouldn't have to feel like I'm hiding and lying all the time.

"Oh! Wow! I guess I guessed wrong, then..." she said, so much calmer than I thought she'd be. She was actually being cool about it! "So, how do you guys know that... How are you sure that you love each other? I mean, you both agree that you do, uh, love each other, am I right?"

"Yeah, Momma. Since last year. Well, about a year ago, anyways," I said.

"I see. So how do you guys... I mean, like, what... Do you hold hands, or kiss, or write each other poems or stuff like that? Help me out here," she smiled, so sweetly and kind. I loved her so much at that moment. I guess it's true that moms are the best, and I felt such a relief.

"Well, yeah, we do that sometimes. I mean, not where anybody can see or anything. We keep it to ourselves," I told her.

"Does Cameron's mom know?"

"No. We don't say or do anything that would make her think—"

"Yeah. That's probably better. So what else do you two get up to?" she asked me. "Have you seen each other...naked, or..."

"Yeah. I mean... We're both, uh..."

"What do you do, then? I can ask! I'm your mom," she smiled. "Go ahead and tell me." I just shrugged my shoulders and kind of stared at my lap. I know she's my mom, but it's still kind of embarrassing, you know?

"Tell you what... How about I ask, and you just nod or shake your head. That way you don't have to say anything." So I nodded. And she asked. Do we touch each other's 'peters'?—I'd never heard it called a peter before! I nodded. Do I know what masturbation is? I nodded. Do we masturbate together? I nodded. Do you masturbate each other? I nodded. Do we play with each other's bottoms? I shook my head 'no'. Do I know what oral sex is? I nodded. Have you done that to Cameron? I nodded. Does he do it to you? I nodded. Do I know what cumming is? I nodded. And she asked do we both cum when we "play around" with each other? I nodded. She finally concluded the interrogation. "Is that everything?" I nodded and looked up at her, hoping to meet tender, understanding eyes.

In the next second I heard the deepest sounding thunks... One! Two! Three! It was the oddest thing. Then everything was like in a movie when you're dreaming and everything's moving fast, but you're in your own, slow world. Then I started hearing slap! slap! slap! and every time I did, my face would move and I could see the blinds on the kitchen wall. But I don't remember turning my head to do it. And the weirdest part: You know what it's like getting thrown upside down into a pool? Well, that's what I imagined was happening, and I couldn't figure out why.

Then I saw Benny and Maisey crying their eyes out! They were in the hallway next to the stairs, and the floor and the stairs were moving, and my arm really hurt at my left shoulder. Kind of just under my armpit. And the next thing I know, I'm face down on the floor of my room. I'm in my room. I'm crying really, really loud, but I somehow can't hear myself. Then I guess I fell asleep.

LATER. (I GUESS IT'S LATER, because it's dark out.) I hear fast, strong steps coming up the stairs. My face is red. And very sore. Bill barges into my room, and his face is as red as mine, only for another reason. He's just angry, and that's how he always looks when he's that way—which is far too often, in my books.

"It's just like I thought from the first time I met your faggot ass!" he screamed. "Well, I'm gonna show you what you deserve, and what you have to

35

look forward to, you little queer!" And then he hit me. He didn't spare the rod, just like his Sunday morning comic book preaches. He yanked my pants down and started wailing on my ass with his dress belt. That's the white, skinny leather belt that makes him look like a disco dancer. It's the church belt.

Whap! Whap! Fucking WHAP! And Whap! again. Do you know that I actually stopped feeling it after about the fifth WHAP? I guess I must have tired his poor Christian arm right out, because when he was done Whapping, he just tossed me against the wall. And that was the worst thing of the whole day so far, because I whiplashed the back of my head against the wall and it hurt like a son of a bitch. It took almost a week for that pain to go away. Then he just left, but not before saying his big exit line: "Now I bet you don't feel so gay, do ya, little girl?!"

I shouted at him, and it was worth it. "Fuck you, you piece of shit! FUCK YOU!" And then I just dissolved into tears while he exacted his last bit of revenge for my honest commentary on his shitiness. As he stormed out of my room, he knocked over my aquarium on purpose. I tried to save them but the fish didn't make it. And the pump that makes their water good was broken. I put them in a plastic Burger King cup so I could show Grampy and

Grammy what he did. "Fuck you, piece of shit asshole!" I screamed down the hall. "Fuck you!"

GRAMPY WAS THERE in about half an hour. I'd snuck into Adolf and Eva's love lair and called him up and told on them. I don't even remember what I said, because when I tried to talk the words tasted funny and sounded rubbery.

My mother came into my room about ten minutes later and—can you believe this—was all cool and acted like nothing had happened. "How ya doing?" she had the fucking nerve to ask me.

"About as good as my dead tropical fish. Get out!"

"Don't talk to me like that, young man!" she barked. "You're going to apologize to Bill for the shit you just said to him, do I make myself clear?!"

"How about fuck off!" I yelled. "The both of you!"

"Okay. I see where this is going!" she blurted out, her lower lip trembling as she wound herself back up again. "Your life is over! You go to school! You go to church! And that is it!"

"We'll see about that, you fucking bitch! I'm not telling you again! Get the fuck out!" and I threw my SpongeBob alarm clock at her. God damn it, I missed! It hit the door jam and poor SpongeBob SquarePants broke into bits.

"I'm not through with you!" she warned. And then left in a huff, quickly pulling my door shut behind her. I lay there trying to calm down and not hurt so much, and then I heard the most wonderful sound in the world!

"WHERE THE FUCK IS HE?!" Grampy demanded. "Where the fuck is my grandson?!" And I heard him practically jumping up the stairs. He burst into my room and saw the destruction. And then he saw me.

Welts from the slapping were already showing on my face, and my butt really, really hurt bad. I told Grampy what they'd done, and he asked where the twins were. I told him I didn't know, and I started crying again. I was saying ow! ow! ow! ow! and he asked what the matter was, and I told him I couldn't lay down or sit down. And I told him my fish were all dead. He rolled me over and pulled my shorts down and saw more red and even some bruises that were starting, and he told me to lay on my side and that he'd be right back. Then he kissed me on my shoulder and I saw he had tears in his eyes.

"Hey!" he shouted, bounding down the stairs, three at a time. "Where the fuck did you cowards go?!"

My mother came around the corner with both of her hands in the air. I call it her Settle Down move. "Daddy! Calm down, Daddy! This doesn't concern you! I don't know what he's told you, but he's in a lotta trouble!"

"Bill!" Grampy shouted. "Come on out here and let's be men, whaddya say, fucker?!" Wow! Grampy cusses with the big words, too! Damn!

I scampered down the stairs just as quick as I could. There was no way I was gonna miss this!

Bill came into the kitchen from the garage. His hair was all messy, and he thought he'd act all tough with Grampy. Big mistake, Idiot Bill! You. Are. So. *Fucked!*

"What the fuck do you want, old man! Get the hell outta my house, asshole!"

Grampy didn't say a word. He grabbed a cast iron skillet off the stove and went after Bill with it, and Bill, piece-of-scared-shitlicker that he is, ran like a girl.

"You're a dead man, fucker! Come here!" Grampy shouted, as they ran round and round from the kitchen to the dining room, to the living room, to the kitchen, and back again. I counted four times before Bill just ran out of the house and closed himself back up in the garage. Grampy threw the skillet against the door and it put about a two-foot gash in it.

Grampy turned to me and told me to go find Benny and Maisey, and to get in his car. Mom started up her shit, but Grampy shut her down quick enough. "Leann, if you say one fucking word... Just one fucking word... I'll have the child services over here so fast that you'll get whiplash. I'd advise you to sit the fuck down and shut the fuck up, little girl!" And she did!

I found the twins huddling in their room, and I took each one by the hand and told them we were going to Grampy and Grammy's house. Then, as we passed by our Mother of the Year, she started up her crap again.

"Make sure you take the car seats with you, and—"

40

"Shut up! Just... Shut up!" Oh, how good that felt. The cool part was, to get the car seats I had to open the garage door, where Fuck Face was hiding out. He kind of jumped a little when the door started to open. But, wise move on his part, he didn't say a word to me as I unstrapped the car seats and carried them to Grampy's wagon. My crowning achievement of the day was when I looked back at him and said, "Later, Big Man!" I hoped he felt as small as his dick.

JOHNNIE IS EIGHTEEN

"BUT YOU CAN'T GO!" Maisey cried.

"Yeah," Benny added, "what if you sink out there on your big boat?"

"I'm not gonna sink, you guys. I'll be fine," I told them. "And Grampy and Grammy say they're gonna check on you every day, and I'll write to you guys and call you all the time." My baby sis and bro were all broken up because I was leaving home to—get this—run away to sea. I was going to work on those big freighters that sail all over the world. I was going away from here. That was the main goal.

I figured that even if this was just going to be a gap year before college, at least I'd have something to show for it. I will have gotten the chance to see the world and be paid for it. Besides, I really needed to get away. And not just because of the Bible thumping duo I was living with.

My heart was broken. Stomped on. Flattened.

My boyfriend, Callum, had betrayed me and I was far from recovering from that little newsflash. I had been with him since the ninth grade, and for the most part had been successful at keeping it on the down low. I didn't avoid who I was, or ever denied who I loved, but I also didn't rub it in my parents' faces either. It was a detente of sorts, and as long as they remained in their fantasy land of Christ hanging out with twelve guys and hanging on a cross, I kept my business to myself.

Callum moved to the States from Canada the summer before ninth grade, and I was attracted to his shyness. He wasn't showy or boisterous, and he was as smart as could be. We liked the same things, and I didn't have to wait very long to see his pink parts because we were on the swim team together.

It was on an away swim meet in Spokane that we first sparked and went through the typical steps it takes for a couple of horny boys to finally end up rolling in the hay. Fake joke #1—completely deniable. Look for his answer. Does he give just a little? Fake question #2—does he bite an even bigger chunk? Then, does he dare me? Or ask me an even more embarrassing "personal" question?

Finally we graduate to tickling and wrestling. We call each other out on our residual boners. "Hey, fag!" "What, fag?" "You're such a fag!" "I dare you to suck me, fag!" "You're too faggy to let me suck you, fag!" "Oh yeah, fag? Well suck this!" And away we go.

The next night, all of the subterfuge is set aside, and we sleep in the same bed, exploring all of the forbidden areas in extremely forbidden ways. The next morning we make sure to mess up the unslept-in bed before sharing a shower and some quick bonus sex before meeting the coach and the rest of the team down in the breakfast room.

Of course months turned into years and our relationship grew. It was a real relationship. I loved him, and he loved me. It was always Johnnie and Callum, Callum and Johnnie. Naturally, I knew my folks suspected the truth; I didn't care. And Callum's family *knew* the truth, and they *didn't* care.

We were good together. We were a team, and I thought we would be for always. But then upped jump the devil, as Grammy would say. I got a phone call from him one night right just after graduation.

Long Before Morning

"Hey, buster blond, can I ask a wee favor?" he purred into the phone.

"Yeah, anything. You know that," I replied.

"Well, I'm going up to Canada to visit my grandparents, but I have a problem that I'm afraid to tell anybody about. And, well..." he said, trailing his words. Yeah, he was embarrassed. So I pressed him a little and he finally told me what was bothering him.

"Johnnie, I just feel so stupid. I got four car payments behind and they're gonna take my car if I don't pay them by tomorrow at five o'clock," he explained with a quiver in his voice. "I need to borrow some money, but if you can do it, well, I'll pay you back. I swear!"

Like he had to worry about something like that. Of course I'd loan him the money. "You wanna meet at my bank in the morning?" I asked him. I could hear the sigh of relief when I told him I'd gladly lend him the dough.

We met outside the bank. I'd already drawn the money out. He'd asked for twenty-two hundred. I'd pulled out twenty-five hundred just in case he needed it for late fees or some such. He was my man. He was my everything. Who cared about money?

Imagine my surprise when I learned three days later that he'd left me for a guy called Pedro who was on the wrestling team. They'd gone to California, and we were no more. I also learned that he didn't even owe anything on his car. His mom and dad had paid for it in full when they bought it for him. Good-bye, Callum. And good-bye twenty-five hundred bucks. So you can imagine I was ripe for going to sea. It was time for a change of scenery, and I was ready to ship out. It would be the best decision I had ever made in my life until then. Thank you, Callum. You can keep the money. We're square. Your cowardly act just brought me that much closer to the life I live now, and the man who's by my side.

PART TWO

SANDER LARS HANSEN

Chapter 2

T

ODAY I'M TURNING three whole years. I

get my own cake. I get some toys. I get my own song. Everybody has to sing it to me—it's the law! *"I dag er det Sander's fødselsdag - hurra, hurra, hurraaaa..."*

Mama woke me up with many kisses, and Pop put a bunch of Danish flags on the walls. And my sister, Ingrid, drew funny pictures of me and already she has said many jokes. So I know this is my birthday!

"Today it is my birthday, did you know that, Mama?"

"Yes! Yes! It's so exciting!" Mama says. "And I bet I have a secret that you don't even know!"

"What's the secret, Mama?" I ask. "You just *have*

to tell me!"

"Well, if I tell you, you must promise to keep it just between you and me."

"I promise! I really do!"

"Okay. Now Sander, do you know why I know that today is your birthday?" she whispers to me.

"No. How do you know? Did *Pop* tell you?"

"I know it is your birthday, because three years ago today I was there when you were born. I was the first person to ever hold you," She explains.

"And *that's* how you know that today it's my birthday?"

"Yes! Because that's what we celebrate. It's the day you were born, and there's nobody else like you in the whole wide world. So we make today a happy day because it's the day that you decided to come down to little Denmark and live with me, and Pop, and your sister too."

"Did I fly down here? Like on a airplane?" I ask. "Was I in the baby plane?"

"Well, your pop is convinced that there were too many princes living at Amalienborg, so the Queen told one of her special guards to find the best family in Denmark and he parked you here. But your pop's a crazy man, so I wouldn't pay much attention to what he says!" Mama smiles.

50

"Hurrah! Hurrah! Hurrah!" says my big sister, skipping into the room. She gives me a big hug and tells me Happy Birthday. She says she is happy that I was born. She says I am the best brother to have. I love Ingrid with my whole heart.

AFTER MY BIRTHDAY PARTY was over I watched a movie about a big whale that escapes from his whale prison. He has a boy called Jesse and a Indian man who is very nice to help him get away. I like movies about whales because whales are very big and jump and are black and white. They live in the sea. I like the boy called Jesse because he is very nice. I wish that he is my friend because I will be a good friend with him if I can. We can play with my Legos and use all of the black and white ones to make a big whale just like in the movie.

It's been a very exciting day but now I'm tired, so I think I'll climb onto Pop and go to sleep on him. He is a good bed. And he pats my bottom and strokes my hair because that's what daddies do. He is good at his daddy job. Mama washes the dishes, and I know when she washes them off with water because

Long Before Morning

I can hear the little water turner-on-er go *sweeeesh.* Then I hear the dishes go *clinky-clank-clonk* and she puts them on the wooden stacker thing for drying. That's what she does.

There's a T.V. in my head, and I can see it when I close my eyes for sleep. Only then can I watch what happens, and it always looks funny. Like my bedroom is very long and has purple walls, and the floor has a stage in the middle of it. My real room has none of these. And I have a funny cat called Boris and he's light green and sings Shu-bi-dua songs.

Then I have a friend who always comes and plays with me in my T.V. He smiles and he talks to me but I can't understand what he says. But I don't care about that because he's so nice to me. He's taller than me but I'm never afraid of him. He has blue eyes like mine, but his hair is yellow. Mine is brown.

This is why I like to sleep. Because many times, when I fall asleep, the yellow-haired boy comes over to play. I told Ingrid about him and she said that he's a dream. But I don't know.

Every time I see him he surprises me. One time he hid behind Boris and then jumped from behind him with a big smile on his face. Boris sang *Askepot,* and me and the yellow-haired boy made things with my Tinkertoys. We made a bridge.

When the yellow-haired boy goes home, I wake up in my bed. Pop carried me here when I was sleeping. It's time for cereal and milk and bread. Then my new day starts. I'm three!

SANDER IS EIGHT

THE BOY LIVES IN ODENSE, DENMARK. Sander Lars Hansen is now a bright kid of eight years. He likes what he likes. He loves who he loves. He reveres animals, as they do him. His family has just bought a semi-detached house that was constructed in late 1976. But the former owners, who had purchased the brick and slate home when it was new, have kept the place immaculate. They even added a carport, and had finished off the upstairs in a large, open plan. There were the two bedrooms — one each for Sander and Ingrid — and the rest of the upstairs loft would serve as the children's playroom. Of course it was nice and exciting to move into a new house.

But there was something each Hansen kid was unaware of. In about six months there would be a third member of the Hansen offspring, and moments after the paperwork was signed and the check handed over, Mama and Pop called the siblings into the center of the living room and invited them to sit campfire style.

"This is your house now," Pop began, grinning ear to ear (which was always funny. Pop's ears moved whenever he talked, but when he smiled he looked a lot like that funny guy on the cover of *Mad Magazine*).

"We are a very lucky family, you know?" Mama added. "Here we have a new house, and the school is just through the common. You can play on the playground anytime you want to."

"And soon enough," Pop continued, "there will be a new playmate for you."

"Who is she?" Ingrid asked with excitement. "Where does she live?"

"We don't know if it's a girl yet," Mama cheerfully explained.

"Then maybe it's a boy," Sander said. "And he can play Legos with me. And Ingrid too."

"Well, maybe it's a boy," Pop chuckled. "One thing is for sure, though. He or she will be living right here." And then the obvious finally reached Ingrid's brain and she shrieked with joy, somewhat startling Sander as she jumped to her feet.

"Do you mean it? Really?!" Ingrid exclaimed. "You're not joking?" Mama and Pop smiled and shook their heads. Sander was confused.

"No, skat, we're not playing around. Mama's got a little baby right there inside of her," Pop said.

"Wait a minute," Sander said. "There will soon be a baby in our house?"

"Yes, Pokey. A whole baby, with a chubby little face and short little legs, and feet as cute as yours!" Mama promised.

"For how long?" Sander asked.

"For how long, what?"

"How long will the baby stay?"

Mom and Pop exchanged confused glances. Ingrid just shrugged as if to say *He's yours! You deal with him.*

"Pokey, I don't think you quite understand that the baby is ours. The baby will live here always. The baby is your little brother or sister," Mama said. "Now do you understand?"

Sander nodded and tears immediately flowed from his big blue eyes. Pop scooped him up and hugged him, as Mama tenderly patted his back. "Honey, what's the matter?"

"What if the baby doesn't like me?" Sander was worried. "What if you don't like me anymore?" And

55

with that he descended into complete, inconsolable sobs.

"Oh, don't ever worry about that, Pokey," Mama promised. "You can worry about all kinds of things but that's one you can never worry about!"

"Sing the song, Mama. Please?" Sander pleaded.

"Will you sing it with me? I will, if you will," Mama smiled. Sander nodded his head and lay his face on Mama's shoulder. He wasn't going to sing. Instead, he would close his eyes and listen to the voice of the one who loved him first.

"Tell me why the ivy twines... Tell me why the stars do shine... Tell me why the sky's so blue... And I will tell you just why I love you!

"...Because our Lord made the stars to shine... Because our Lord made the ivy twine... Because our Lord made the sky so blue... Because He made you, that's why I love you..."

The boy was asleep, an angel on her shoulder. She crept up the stairs and laid him gently on the floor, covering him with a painter's drop cloth. He smiled when she kissed him on his forehead, and then cuddled with the plush toy he never went anywhere without—an elephant named Holger. And as he drifted away, he dreamed about a small boy who held his hand and called him Brother.

SANDER IS FIFTEEN

IT'S BEEN A YEAR SINCE that day that I was stupid. A guy that I loved broke my heart, I got very emotional, and I tried to end my life. That was very dumb, especially when you stop and think that my little brother was the one who walked in and really ended up saving my life.

Now I have to see the head shrinker. I'm supposed to get to the bottom of why I got so upset that I wanted to hurt myself. Thing is, sure, I was sad that Torben broke up with me. I love him. But the reason I was so sad was because the kids at school hit me, and spat on me, and threw my things into the sewer. And, well, I really don't want to re-imagine it all over again. Besides, they each apologized to me, and said they were sorry. Why can't we just move on?

My parents act like they don't know what to do with me. Pop won't let me out of his sight. Don't tell anyone, but I know I'm his favorite. And while I know I upset Jannik, it just about killed my father. I've never seen him cry so much and for so long. I really feel bad about that.

I've fallen into a hole. I've got to find my way out of it. Maybe this year will be different. I'm supposed

57

to go with Georg to a party at his brother's apartment building. It's really cold outside, and I don't know if I want to fight the snow. Maybe I'll go.

OKAY, I DECIDED TO GO TO the stupid party. I didn't even know what it was for, not that you really have to have a reason for a party. My friend Bo said it was for a new guy who moved in to the building. He's from America, so it'll be interesting to see the American. Also, Bo promised he'd bring some really good weed so there's that.

The place is packed. I guess everyone wanted to see the American, too. As usual, Emma—she's the old gal who watches over the place—has the heat up too high. A perfect excuse to grab a couple of appelsin sodas (they taste like oranges from Florida!) out of the big ice bucket. Bo finally taught me the trick on how to open one bottle with the other bottle. Of course, idiot boy (me!) got it wrong and I caused it to explode all over me. Everybody laughed and I got all sticky and now I smell like a citrus tree. And of course, I did this all in front of the American.

The American.

He's really tall, and he's really fine. I mean, I can't take my eyes off of him. And every time I look his way he catches me. He probably thinks I'm a stalker freak. And his hair! It's so yellow, and he's got the kindest face. They say that Americans are loud and kind of—dumb's not the word—kind of uneducated about other cultures. This guy—I think his name is John—isn't that way at all. Oh, God! I just saw his crotch! Fuck, either he stuffs sausages down there or he's packing some heat!

"Hi, I'm called Sander Lars Hansen," I say to him. Oh my God, you should see his smile! "Welcome to Denmark."

"Thank you! I'm so happy I'm here. Look, I saw you got drenched in orange juice there, come here. Let's clean it up a little," he said, as he gently guided me to the sink. He was so very sweet. I'm glad I came to the party. I just caught a glimpse of his butt. Now I know why they invented blue jeans. It's so that perfect butts have a place to live and show the rest of us how a perfect butt is supposed to look.

"You don't have to do this," I told him.

"I don't mind a bit," he said.

"The party's for you. You should be...partying!" That made him laugh. That was the first time I heard

Johnnie Paul Allen laugh. It hopefully wouldn't be the last.

"Nah! It's not for me, it's a winter solstice party. That's what Emil told me," he said. "Why would they have a party for me?"

"Because you are the big news around here, and because solstice was a month ago?" I told him. I turned quickly to my right so his hand with the wiping cloth would rub past the left side of my butt. He touched my butt! Yes! Sander Hansen, bridging the cultural gap for Queen and Country! Now how can I get him to brush past the lump growing behind my zipper?

"Are you here for the school?" I asked Johnnie. He told me he would be taking nothing but Danish classes for the whole year, and he said I'd be welcome over at his place anytime. "Especially if you want to help me with my Danish," he laughed.

"What is the number of your flat?" I asked him.

"Number eleven. On the ground floor. It's the one with the yellow-haired Yank behind the door," he smiled.

"Ah! *That* number eleven. Okay, now I know!" I replied. And now the very good looking American was officially my new friend. That was some great news for me. The bad news? I couldn't stop thinking about him. Damn! There's his butt again!

––––––––––––––––––––––––––––––––

LATER THAT SAME NIGHT—it was really late— and I didn't get home from the party until two-thirty. Then I had to walk to every room in the house and make sure everything was fine. I can't help that. I always have done this, and now I learn it's called an obsessive compulsive act. There's names for everything now. I prefer to think it's because I need to know that everybody in my wolf pack is okay, and that they're secure. I just think it's because I love my family.

I'm downstairs and so I check Mama and Pop's room first. They always sleep with their door wide open. They always have, so they can check on us and know that we're safe. I know they're okay because Pop's snoring makes the walls shake.

Next is Ingrid. I slowly open her door and see her all bundled up in her eiderdown. She's alone tonight; no boyfriend.

Next door to my room is the nursery. That's what it's still called even though Jannik is already in klasse two at school. He's my buddy. He sleeps so sweetly. He moved his bed against the wall next to my bed and sometimes he taps out messages for me to hear. It's like we're in a prison movie, or one of those films where we're in a World War II jungle Japanese prison camp and we're British soldiers. He always taps out the same thing: Take Your Quinine. He's smart, and he's the best brother I could ever have. I love him so much.

I lay down on my comfortable, cozy bed. I remember when I got it. It was when we first moved here and Pop said we were giving all of our old beds away to the Lutherans, and we could pick out new ones at Thomsen's Møbler. I laid on this bed in the store and I liked it right away. Old man Thomsen smiled at me and said I couldn't take the bed until I tried out one very important thing. Mama asked him what it was, and he smiled and took my hand, standing me up on the bed. "Okay, now jump!" he told me. Pop just laughed and said, yes, it's very important to know how high I could jump on the bed since we would be friends for a very long time.

Pop opened his arms wide, and on my last, highest jump I aimed for him. He caught me and held me in his arms. "Well, Thomsen, what do you think?" Pop asked. Thomsen was already writing up the sale.

I'm thankful for my family. I closed my eyes and made the peaceful transition to the other world I visit on so many nights in my eiderdown-cloaked space ship.

I'm in my room and there are Legos on the floor. In the corner is my friend. He's the boy with the yellow hair. He turns and looks my way, his big-toothed grin telling me it's time to play. I recognize him. I scoot onto the floor, my knees buried in the thickly padded Berber carpeting, and I hug him. "Hi, Johnnie," I say, and then I ask him what we're going to build today. My eyes lock on his and I know at once that he has always been my friend, and that he always will be.

PART THREE

EUGENY ANTONOVICH KUZMICH

Chapter 3

EUGENY IS BORN

EUGENY ANTONOVICH KUZMICH, quite

an unexpected gift for his mother and father, entered the world on December 26, 1991, which was the first day of the new Russian Federation.

At 7:32 p.m. the night before—Christmas day— the blood red cloth with the golden hammer and sickle, representing the newly extinct Union of Soviet Socialist Republics, was lowered at the Kremlin for the last time. The baby boy would never know life in his country as it had been for his grandfather, or the great grandparents who were there when the USSR was born, or even for his own mother and father, who were more excited by the prospect of ample foodstuffs lining the market shelves, or the durable goods that were undoubtedly not far behind, than by witnessing history that mere months before could have never been imagined. The Kuzmich family was eager for western music on compact discs, and the hundreds of liquor choices soon to come. Yeah, the kid was cute and all, but babies are babies and stuff is, well, *stuff.*

Anton Kuzmich was a run-of-the-mill factory worker—a machinist by trade—and his girlfriend, Elena, was a secretary at a grammar school. They met when Anton was picking up a little black work by helping a friend install a new heating system. Elena had been tasked to monitor the men's work. She had done an especially good job monitoring Anton, because nine months later out popped Eugeny.

"What do we do now?" she asked her boyfriend. "I hear that all of the programs are dissolved. How do we get milk, and heat, and things for the baby—how do we eat?" Her concern was legitimate.

"Leave him with your mother," he suggested. "And we'll find a place to move where we can get good jobs and afford to pay for these things.

Otherwise we land on the road like half of everybody else in this fucking country. If it's even a country now."

When she would dare contradict him on any point at all—reality was not one of Anton's strong suits—he would end up exploding at her and huffing off to find a true friend who might come equipped with a vodka bottle.

"Why do you wish to be the fucking Russian stereotype, asshole?!" she would shout after him. He'd have to take it for twelve stair flights down because none of the elevators in the building worked anymore, and then all the way across the green space between apartment blocks. The neighbors would be privy to it, too. But then, they were very well-versed in the subject of the neighbors and their own dirty laundry.

"Piss off, you dozy crone! I don't need any of your shit!" And then he'd round the corner, not to be seen again until the morning. She would slam the door, the neighbor to the right would indignantly yell, "Hey!" and then she'd change Eugeny's diaper and heat up some soup and tea. Thus was the groundhog's day lifestyle she would endure until she finally found the courage six years later to leave the bastard and pick up stakes for Kiev. Ukraine would be the answer, she just knew it. It was common knowledge that the Ukrainian economy was expanding by leaps and bounds, and she might even eventually find her way to the Czech Republic if she played her cards right.

So with Eugeny and two battered suitcases, Elena Sofia Annakolvina Kuzmich boarded the *Stolichny Express* at Moscow's Kiyevsky Station, and settled in for the overnight train ride to her future.

EUGENY IS ELEVEN

UKRAINIAN SUMMER IS A combination of moist, humid, bug-laden heat with the occasional downpour. It's rain good for nothing more than causing traffic accidents and discovering more roof repair spots that have opened up since the last deluge. It was in such a storm that Eugeny found himself as he ran from the Nikolai Gogol Intermediate School, to the ramshackle hovel he and his mother call home.

Always clever and resourceful, Eugeny followed a route of his own design that would ensure passing a number of shops and vegetable markets ripe for pilfering his evening meal. But every time an afternoon drenching like this one took place, it would interfere with his larcenous plans. This is because he relied on a marketplace full of rabid shoppers to provide cover while he relieved the many vendors of a few free samples. Today the rain kept the babushkas home with their malodorous husbands, which meant that if he wanted to eat he'd either have to create a diversion, or become much more brazen, thereby exceeding his comfort level.

"You! Boy! Come here!" the butcher with the lambs and the pigs shouted. "Do you think I'm playing fun?! Come here now!"

Momentarily confused, Eugeny found himself pulled toward the squat, gray-haired man holding the meat cleaver. "What do you want?" Eugeny demanded.

"I have a proposition for you. And you either do what I say, or you sleep in the jail tonight."

"I'm listening," Eugeny replied.

"Come closer. I'm not going to holler my business to all of these nosy assholes!" the man hissed. "Come here!"

The boy complied, cautious at first, but still remained just out of reach in case this audience turned against him. "Okay. What do you want?" Eugeny asked.

"It's very simple," the butcher explained. "I know who you are. I know where you live. I know that your mother works at the Lada factory. And I know how much you steal from us honest vendors in the marketplace." The lanky pre-teen remained silent, choosing instead to exercise the better part of valor. He shrugged his shoulders.

"Ah! So that's how it will be. I see," the man stated. "Fine! Move along, but you can expect a visit from the police."

"What do you want?"

"I have a job for you."

"So you say. What kind of a job?" Eugeny asked.

"The kind where if you keep your mouth shut, you can make more money than you ever imagined. And then you can pay us for the things you take," the butcher explained, chopping up some pig legs for later pickling. "But I must warn you. If you ever breathe a word of this to anyone... *Anyone!*"

"I'm not a fink!" Eugeny protested. "You will see!" And as if on cue, the rotund butcher slammed his cleaver onto the pig's neck, severing the head.

EUGENY BURST INTO THE ONE room shack on Petrovsky Common and preened to his mother. He dropped a sack of meat—of which kind, he wasn't exactly sure—and shot her a little smile. Then he opened his coat and revealed a plastic bag stuffed with potatoes and, of all things, three oranges from Crimea.

"What is all this?" his mother asked.

"It is food. You eat it and live to shit another day," he answered cheekily. "I get it for us at the market. I have a job now," Eugeny explained.

"What kind of job?" she demanded.

"The kind where we eat. That's all you need to know."

"I beg your pardon?"

"Beg all you want, it's my business. Now cook if you want an evening meal. If not, that's fine too!" he shot back at her. "I'll hear no more about it!" And with that, he disappeared behind the curtain that was the only demarcation line of privacy in the dingy grayness of the apartment.

Long Before Morning

THE BUTCHER TOLD EUGENY that if he broke into a converted warehouse in the Petro Distrikt, and successfully transferred ownership of three ammo boxes of AK cartridge upgraded penetrables—fancy bullets that laugh at a cop's armored vest—into his exclusive custody, the boy would receive enough money to live like a Tsar for three months.

"What if I get caught?" Eugeny asked.

"Then I promise I'll pay for your funeral," came the terse reply. "Do it by Saturday because I have a customer." The butcher waved him away, but before he did, Eugeny nodded. He took the job.

"You better not fuck me over," Eugeny warned as he walked away. "Because I'm not the only one who looks good in a coffin." The butcher couldn't help smiling at the teen's fearless display of bravado. This kid just might work out, he thought.

EUGENY IS EIGHTEEN

EIGHTEEN IS A GOOD AGE. When you're eighteen it seems that people listen—somewhat, anyway. By now Eugeny had built quite the reputation. He was nine years on the job and completely embedded in Russian organized crime. He'd crossed the line into murder—that happened when he was fourteen—and he had thirteen confirmed kills on his belt. Yeah, they were mostly lowlife pimps, drug dealers, and arms merchants, but they were still human. They had families. But none of that mattered to Eugeny as long as the cash arrived on time.

He fooled around with a counterfeit operation once, back when he was sixteen (two whole years ago!), and that association almost got him killed. But it all evened out when he took the contract from a rival crime syndicate to off the man who had almost killed him.

His mother was in the long-term hospital with a debilitating case of rheumatoid arthritis, and he was determined to make enough money someday to get her transferred to someplace in the west that could actually do her some good. In his mind, she had just been parked in a government warehouse. The doctors didn't really do anything to help her, and the nurses were just psychopaths. Mean bitches and even bitchier fags. He fantasized about walking in there with an AK and spraying bullets like a gun nutty American on a college campus. Sweet revenge.

Long Before Morning

"Hey, Stalin!" the butcher shouted. "Come here!" Eugeny had been known by his associates and peers as Stalin since he kidnapped a banker's family and held them until the bank fulfilled the ransom demand of all of the Euros, dollars, and yen that the bank had on hand. The bank wouldn't budge, and when the deadline passed... Well, there's a reason they're called *dead*lines. When Eugeny got the word that it was a no-go with the bank, he ended the lives of the wife, two grade school-age sons, and an infant daughter with less thought than taking out the trash. Stalin means 'steel', and his lack of empathy for the victims or the grieving bank manager was about as steely as it comes. He even got a bonus for disappearing the corpses of the once vibrant family. His take? About eleven hundred U.S. dollars.

"What is it?" Eugeny asked the butcher. "I'm off to hospital."

"Not today you aren't. Today you go see the Jew about a hundred cars that have gone missing."

"A hundred cars? Shit, man, that's a lot of cars. Where are they missing from?" Eugeny asked.

"I don't know. Wherever you take them from. The Jew's got a huge sack of cash he wants to pay you, so I would go and see him if I was you. Or don't, and wish he don't get mad," the butcher said.

"Fuck! I hate that fucker! And that sack of cash you talk of will be smaller than your dick. I told you I don't want to work for that maggot again!" Eugeny spouted off. "I mean it!"

"Oh! You *mean* it! Well that changes everything!" the butcher responded sarcastically. "Get over to the Jew now, or you'll have more than him to worry about!" the butcher yelled. Eugeny stormed off, mad as hell. But he knew there was nothing he could do about it. That's the downside of his particular occupation. Once you're all in, you're *all in.*

PART FOUR

RETURN TO PRESENT DAY

Chapter 4

JOHNNIE AND SANDER

THE CALL FROM THE assignment desk

came in saying I had about two hours before a detail would arrive at our front door to collect me for the ride into Copenhagen. We live about an hour and forty minutes from central Copenhagen, on the island of Fyn. It's so beautiful here.

"So what does it mean?" Sander asked with marked concern in his voice. "This is the first time they've been so quick. I mean, there's no notice and I wonder if you'll be okay. Should I worry?"

"No. Don't worry any more than usual. It's just a typical—"

Long Before Morning

"Don't say that! It's *not* typical and I know it's not! *You* know it's not, so don't treat me like a kid, okay?!" Sander exclaimed. "Do you even know what it is?"

"No. I mean, it can only be one of a couple of things. You know that. And there aren't really that many hot spots to think about, anyway," I said, doing my best to reassure this tender man who loves me so very much that all would be well. I couldn't bear the thought of him losing sleep, or not being able to think about anything other than my job trip. "You know I'll call when I can, or leave little sugar bombs on my Facebook for you," I told him, doing my best to act like none of this was any big deal.

"You don't know what it's like, though," Sander argued. "Last time they sent you to fucking Africa on a goddamned submarine. You know how far away that was? And just like then, they won't tell you anything till you get to Copenhagen—and the next time we'll hear anything is when you're wherever-the-fuck you go!"

I looked him in the eyes—those beautiful, sparkling ice blue eyes that guard the most tender and loving soul—and leaned into him, mating my lips to his, and kissed his sweet face for what felt like time stopped. He pulled back and smiled.

"Johnnie?"

"Yeah?" I breathed. I caught a whiff of the intoxicating smell of his Blue Stratos cologne, mixed with the freshness of his clothing. It filled the room.

"We have some time. Not much. But—"

I took his hand and squeezed it three times, then followed him to our cozy bedroom. Within seconds we were down to our shorts and climbing under the eiderdown, the room illuminated by a single candle placed on the northern sill.

"I want you to know how I feel about you right now. You have to remember this, yeah?" Sander whispered to me. "There are only so many times that 'I love you' can be said before I have to show you what that means," he smiled.

"I never get tired of hearing it," I said. "Ever..."

"Then I hope you'll never get tired of this," he said, positioning himself to pull off my underwear, then quickly tossing it over the foot of our bed.

"Pokey, you know that you're the only thing on my mind whenever I'm gone, right?" I said.

"Yep. Even when you're on a submarine full of hot looking navy guys, I know." he joked. "But I still need to give you something to come home for, and this is it," he explained, and then took my hardening cock into his mouth and gently brought it to full staff with his soft lips and ready tongue.

"Oh, fuck! That's good. Jesus fucking Christ in a whorehouse, how the fuck do you do that?" I asked with a tremor in my voice. He just carried on, slowly picking up speed and zeroing in on that rhythmic timing he knows I like.

As soon as we were in sync with each other, he began to explore my ass with his fingers, every so often brushing his hand up against my balls.

I hugged his legs and scooted him closer to me, repositioning just enough so I could take his stiffened manhood into my own mouth and begin returning the pleasures he so freely and lovingly gave me.

We pleased each other orally for a good half hour when the familiar stirrings of my need to feel him inside me took hold.

"Sander, can you..." I began. And before I could expel the sentence he rolled over, gently directed me face down on the bed, and began to orally stimulate my sensitive and waiting ass. His tongue sought and explored places not spoken of, while reaching under me to encircle my hard cock with his hand. He stroked me as his tongue continued to bring unbelievable pleasure up and down my ass crack, and then in a singular motion pulled himself onto me.

I felt his warm breath against my neck, and in one gentle thrust he was inside me. The feeling of his beautiful penis as it entered and became, for a time, part of me, is the ultimate expression of his love.

"Does it feel fine, Johnnie?" he asks me, as if my moans of passion and unrestrained pleasure aren't enough to answer his question.

"Oh, so good, Sander. So wonderful!" I tell him. "Fuck me! Make love to me, sweet prince! My God, I love you so much!" I stammer.

"Wow! I'm royalty now!" he chuckles. "I can like this very much!"

As the crescendo approached, he doubled his speed, and it just felt fantastic. I could feel his foreskin retract on every inward push, and the stimulation of the outward pulls raised his breathing, which only turned me on more. Then he pulled the surprise move that still gets me hard every time my mind drifts to it.

At the height of his passionate and demonstrative lovemaking, he reached underneath me and grasped my dick, rolling us together onto our left sides. He never missed a single thrust as he began stroking and jerking my hard, throbbing cock to orgasm. He managed about five more minutes of this before his rapid heartbeat and quickening breath signaled the release that he was about to impart.

My balls slapped in rhythm as he jacked me to within seconds of my own pending blast. Then I felt him fill my ass with his warm nectar. Once again, Sander Lars Hansen had joined with me. Once again, the proof of his deep love for me lay inside me. And at that moment, when my love for him could not possibly be any stronger, I released my semen all over his hand, fingers, my belly, and our bed. And as soon as he backed the furious stroking down to a slow, light motion, he brought the side of his hand to his lips and took my cum into his mouth.

"I love you, Johnnie," he said, rolling onto his back. "I love you too goddamned fucking much!" he continued, "You're like crack to me! Or pizza!" he laughed.

"Or custard?" I joked, pulling on his lower lip.

"You taste better than custard," He smiled. "Way better!"

We lie there as long as we can, and then the pending arrival of my ride dictates that we rejoin the world. "What do you need to pack?" Sander asks, pulling his underwear along his perfect thighs, and up over his ass.

"I'm just gonna take my scramble bag," I tell him. "There's plenty of clothes in it; some snacks, waters, tools. Why fuck with more?" I reason.

"What about Jannik?" he asks me. "What do I tell him? And everybody else?"

"I'll call him when I get to the embassy, and just let everybody know it's just a typical trip. I'm probably just filling in for somebody else anyways. I'm sure that's why I got the short call," I explain.

"Okay. Well, let's go wait for the guys then. Want a bowl of ice cream?" Sander offers.

"Damn straight! Lots of nuts, too! And some whipped cream."

"That sounds way to sexual, Johnnie Bond. Way too sexual."

NO SOONER HAD WE TAKEN A SEAT on the romper couch, than a stiff knock on the door assaulted our peaceful afterglow. No mistaking a government knock.

"I get it!" Sander announced, springing for the door. "I think your ride is here."

"What if we hide in the bathroom?" I chuckled. "Maybe they'll give up and piss off."

"Hey, guys!" Sander smiled as he opened the door. "He's in here. Just a little minute. Come, please, inside." He led the two embassy marines to the kitchen table and offered them chairs, coffee, and snacks. "Have a coffee or a Coke or something, yeah? If you both is driving my man all whole way to Copenhagen this late on the night, we can't have you to be falling asleep, yes?"

Sander did his best, but he worried that his English wasn't up to par—something he is always concerned about no matter what the situation—and he especially wanted to prove to the impressive American military men that he wasn't some simpleton who was only capable of communicating in overly accented pidgin English. They heard him, though. They understood. Especially about the "driving my man" part. The shorter of the two, Lance Corporal Dave Kimball, didn't try to mask his disgust at us fags living together out in the Danish countryside. So it must have struck his homophobic straightness right in the nuts when Sander and I shared a passionate good-bye kiss. His buddy, Private First Class Luis Gonzalez, at least had the class to look past us and fix his eyes on the Bailey Skater original painting hanging above our fireplace.

"Bye, Pokey, I love you," I told Sander, a lump rising where I don't like lumps to rise—my throat. "See you when I see you!"

The tears welled in his eyes as he grabbed my bag and walked quickly to the car. "Not if I see you first!" he said, trying his best to bring a little mirth to our forced farewell. "Write if you find work!" he joked.

Long Before Morning

I couldn't bear to look back at the house as we headed down the drive to the main road. So I just kept myself focused on the glow of the lights of our tiny town of Gelsted up ahead, and settled in for the ride. There was nothing more to do.

Chapter 5

I LOVE DENMARK just as much as any Dane

wandering the streets of Copenhagen. By now I even consider myself more than as an honorary Dane. But something stirs whenever I approach the American Embassy, especially at night, and see the Stars and Stripes snapping overhead, bathed in a constant light. I think it is one of the most beautiful flags in the world, and for all of our many faults, I'm proud of where I come from.

"We'll drop you at the kitchen entrance because your meeting's in the Ambassador's Dining Room," Lance Corporal Kimball informed me. "We'll take your scram bag to that van you see over there past the playground. Good luck."

"Thanks. And thanks for the lift, guys," I said, softly shutting the car door to stave off the hellacious noise it would make, the sound bouncing and echoing off the security walls and concrete buildings. I'd made that mistake once before and had heard about it later.

The porch light outside the kitchen cast an eerie glow, as by now a fog had rolled in across the Øresund from Sweden. It likely wouldn't burn off until noon tomorrow. I heard voices and the clinking of coffee cups in sync with the gurgling urn filling the room with its enticing aroma of boiling Arabica beans. Rounding the corner of the waiters' exit into the ornate dining room, I was surprised to see how many people were here. What's more, the ranking of those I recognized proved this was more than an ordinary asset delivery.

"Johnnie! Man of the hour," said my boss and good friend Marguax Stuplemann. "It's about time!" she kidded.

"So you're the one who yanked me outta bed! I shoulda known," I teased. "I swear, if my day ever goes lopsided I know who's the responsible party."

"Shut up and take a seat, kid. You're not too big to take over my knee!" she shot back.

"Marge! I'm sure there's some H.R. Regs that'll keep you from doing that, fun as it may sound," came the comment from the handsome gentleman at the end of the table.

"Ah, Rufus, I changed his diapers. Johnnie, meet Rufus Gifford. Ambassador Gifford, Johnnie Allen. He's the groundhog for this mission. And there's none better," Marge said.

"I know who he is, Marge. Your reputation precedes you, Mr. Allen," the ambassador said. "Okay, everybody, I'll leave it to you. I need to leave the meeting now that everybody's here. That pesky 'plausible deniability' thing'll getcha every time. Goodnight."

"Goodnight, sir."

"Sir."

"Goodnight, Mr. Ambassador."

"'Night, Rufus!" (You can guess who said that.) "Okay, Johnnie. Pay attention to the nice man with the funny accent," Marge declared.

"You're sure cheeky with the ambassador," I whispered to Marge. "That's the president's handpicked rep, and you act like you're his mom or something!" I chuckled.

"In a way I am!" she hissed back at me.

"What?"

"He's family," she reported, averting my eyes to avoid the church laugh I could see building inside her.

"What do you mean, 'family'," I demanded, my own insides starting to tickle a bit.

"You know, he's...*family*."

"You mean..."

"Yep. Makes *you* look straight as a jock," she told me, biting her lip and doing her best to not give in to the mirthful force begging to escape her now-shaking body.

"You mean he's queer as a..."

"If you fucking say one more word, you're a dead gay boy, Johnnie Allen. I swear on my bulbous ass, I'll god damned wring that blond neck of yours, sure as I'm a lesbian in heat," Marge promised. "Now look at the handsome Dane while I try and recover what dignity I still have."

The Dane she referred to happened to be the head of the P.E.T., Denmark's own C.I.A. I remembered him from Operation Mango. He was the guy who helped Marge coordinate what amounted to my and Sander's rescue after I had totally screwed up my first assignment in every imaginable way. Even to the point of losing our vehicle—a swank BMW—to an embedded Russian operative who had impersonated the asset we were supposed to deliver to a waiting cargo vessel in Antwerp. If it hadn't been for Marge and Colonel Jens Jespersen, these journals I write would have suddenly ended halfway through the first one. For good.

"Colonel Jespersen, I'm honored to see you again. I never had the chance to thank you," I told him.

"Well, you buy me a beer when this is all over and we'll call it even," he said. To say I was intrigued by whatever 'this' was is a gross understatement.

"First, I'm happy that everyone made it here in one piece, and on time. This is not my mission, but because it launches from Denmark, I'm at least involved in the 'Need to Know' part of everything. Consider us your hosts. And of course, your haven once Dutch Oven is successfully executed," Jespersen began.

So. It has a code name. 'Dutch Oven'. Yeah, this wasn't your average day at work, that's for damned sure. "I think, in the name of expediency, it's best that I turn this over to Major Vanderman of Netherlands Special Forces, and Captain Lanning of British SAS. Gentlemen..." Jespersen concluded.

An orderly turned the lights down and the mission specifics appeared on a screen lowered from the white and gold-leafed rococo ceiling. A tad better than a typical PowerPoint presentation, when I learned what we would be doing, and the logistics involved for it to succeed, I confess that I was so excited by it all that, well, let's just say I had to adjust the front of my underpants a little.

"Who remembers the date seventeenth July of last year?" asked the Dutch major. "Don't be shy. I want to know if anyone other than my team remembers what happened on that day."

Marge looked in my direction, catching my eye while nodding her head towards the major. She knew that I knew.

"Sir?" I raised my hand.

"Yes, uh, Johnnie is it?"

"Sir, Malaysian Flight MH-17 was shot down over Ukraine. Sir."

"Yes," he agreed. "And with it, hundreds of Dutch citizens, and a sizeable roster of British and Aussies; some three dozen of them. And more innocent civilians just minding their own business, flying along on a commercial airliner."

The major explained that just two weeks prior to this briefing, a serious multinational proposition to the United Nations requesting a resolution to set up an international tribunal for prosecuting the suspects responsible for downing the airliner was proposed. It was vetoed by the Chair of the U.N. Security Council. Who was it? "It was vetoed by Russia," the major declared. "And that didn't sit well with us."

"Or us," added SAS Captain Lanning.

"So, the time has come for the butcher's bill to be paid," the major continued. "And we've been charged with collecting on it."

Wait a minute. Wow. So Putin was about to be majorly spanked. He had no clue that the personnel gathered in this room at the American Embassy in little Denmark were about to conjure the wrath of hell upon his beady eyes and blackened heart.

"Gentlemen and lady, I want to make it perfectly clear that no nation on this planet can murder two hundred ninety-eight souls in the name of a proxy war and have that crime go unpunished," the major stated emphatically.

"Mr. Putin will rue the day that he ever was involved in this mischief, and our mission is to teach him this lesson by ending his shooters' existence. His Majesty and his entire government wish to send a clear message to the Kremlin that the days of its wanton disregard for human decency are over."

"SO WHEN CAN WE LEAVE?" Captain Lanning asked me, as bluntly as any SAS captain hailing from Manchester would do. "I do hope there's no paralysis by analysis going on here. That wouldn't do at all."

"No, Captain Lanning. I promise you that you're gonna get in and out, safe and sound. That's what I do," I told him.

"I dunno why we just can't zip in, zip out, and be bloody done with it. Everything's always got to be such a big production with you Yanks," he added.

"Sir, with all due respect, I don't want an Operation Ellamy on my watch. Sir." Okay, now I'd done it. "You and your men deserve more. So if you don't mind..."

"What the bloody hell do you know about it? You're a fucking child!" he barked.

"E-Squadron! Remember that? You don't deserve it, and my age has nothing to do with it. Not one fucking thing!" I could give as good as I get. "It was a failure, and it wasn't your fault! It was the insertion! And if I'm wrong and full of shit, then take it up with my superior. But god damn if I'm not gonna do everything I can to make sure that it doesn't happen here!"

Whenever I get angry, which isn't often, my face turns red as a traffic light. And against my yellow blond hair makes me look like a Dr. Seuss character. The captain just stared at me for what felt like an hour, then quickly shot off a "Very well. Let me know as soon as you know. Carry on."

He reached the corridor outside the dining room and just lost it in the biggest burst of laughter I'd heard in a very long while. I must have really looked a sight. Fuck. There I go again, winning friends and influencing people. I've got to work on my bedside delivery, I guess. But I meant what I said.

Back in 2011, when Libya was the latest middle eastern headache, the SAS were sent into Benghazi along with a diplomat who was supposed to assess the situation on the ground. But it was done with absolutely no insertion plan. None. So when the chopper touched ground they were met by local militia who weren't all that happy to see them.

Considering that the helicopter had landed in the dead of night, with no warning, blacked out, with a contingent of SAS dressed in black, who had ironically just sprayed "warning shots" over the heads of the local town folk—well, do you understand the picture I'm trying to paint here?

That's why I stood up to the captain. The last thing he needs is an appearance in *Benghazi: The Sequel*. That contingency of SAS professionals found themselves tossed into a local jail until cooler minds prevailed and they were finally allowed to flee aboard *HMS Cumberland*. Tails were definitely between legs on that day.

"Johnnie Allen, I hear good reports of your resolute planning." I looked up from my geo-report software program to catch the erudite form of Ambassador Gifford. "This all going to happen the way they need it to?" he asked.

"I'll get them safely in and out, Mr. Ambassador. That's about all I can promise."

"What's your timeframe?" he asked.

"After it's in good shape I'll meet with the brass, and provided they think it's a good plan, I'll need less than twenty-four hours to get all my props ready and we're off," I told him.

"Anything you need from the embassy?" he asked.

"The graphics shop is gonna be a little overrun, and State and maybe the British Consul will have to issue some working passports that look well-worn and beat up. Otherwise, expense and graft money, and a gasoline credit card or two and we're good to go," I promised. "And all that's only if the Brits and the Dutch okay my delivery and egress plans."

"Here, go find one of the loaner offices," he said, handing me a master key with an embossed state department logo. The privacy would be appreciated. "Drop the key through the Visa Department's mail slot when you're done, and if I miss you before you go, good luck."

"Thank you, sir." I said. Gifford glided out of the room as quietly as he'd entered, stopping to flick off unnecessary lights and checking that the kitchen door was locked.

"SOUNDS GOOD TO US, mate," was the consensus in the room. I'd spent the better part of an hour outlining the proposed timetable, and they were universally enthusiastic in their assessments of it. Now it was time to put it all into motion.

"You need two of these, big enough for a panel van? What the hell?" said the manager of the embassy's graphics and printing shop. "And you want'em in a hour? You think you at Kinko's or somethin'?"

Tyrone Johnson and I always go through this every time I need him to whip up some legend for me on his graphics table. Marge and I call it the Tyrone Dance. It goes something like this...

I say *Hi, Tyrone,* and he looks at me like death crossed his threshold with a black cloak and a scythe. Then he goes *Mhmmm* in his best *I don't give a shit who you think you are* Detroit attitude. And then I act like I didn't see him do that and say some self deprecating line like, *Look, it's me, your favorite privileged suburbanite never-got-stopped-by-a-cop white boy!*

Then Tyrone kind of smirks like, *God damn it, Johnnie, don't make me laugh.* Then he says, *Not that I'm gonna do it, but what the fuck it is you need yesterday, you white devil?* That's when I know I've won and my timetable will be met.

"I knew you could do it. See, this is a really important assignment and the legend has to be perfect. It's critical," I say.

"Mhmmm. Cuz the last fifty-two of 'em weren't," he glibly reminds me. To which I start defending the life or death importance of this-- "Come back in a hour. Bring me weed. And none-a-that bullshit German crap. Drive your tasty little white ass over to Christania and get me the good shit," he smiles. "I'll

102

have your lil' project here all done up when you get back."

Dang! That was easy. Cool.

IT'S T-MINUS TWO HOURS ELEVEN and I'm putting the finishing touches on the van graphics Tyrone made for me. It depicts a van full of roughneck oil workers heading east to Ukrainian oil fields. Tyrone is helping me distress the signs. They need to look like they've been on this ugly-ass van since baby Bush stole the 2004 election from Al Gore.

While we put the Hollywood touches on the van, the special forces gents are changing into their smelly, dirty oil field overalls and work boots. This they do right here out in the open, all traces of any military association—insignia, ID cards, even nationalities—completely removed and placed inside personal rucksacks to be stowed here at the embassy until our return.

"Where's those front and rear window placards?" I ask Tyrone.

"They inside, like you said," he responds. "Ain't that what you say to do with 'em?"

"Perfect. Come here. Walk with me," I say, "over by the livery." We move behind the van and cross the open drive to the motor pool. The guys are still kitting out and talking to each other a mile a minute, which gives me the chance to buy a little insurance. "Those placards you made. I need you to do something with 'em that, no lie, is so important that if you don't do it tomorrow it might...well, let's just say things could really go wrong for these guys," I tell him.

"What is it? I'm in. You know that, White Pain," he smiled. "For serious!"

"I know you are. That's why I'm asking you."

"Right. So tell a brother..."

"I need you to send those placards by regular mail first thing in the morning. And these keys. Send them here," I say, passing him a name and address scratched on the back of a dining hall menu card. "But it's gotta be first thing. You can't wait even a day, because I need them to get there in time."

"I can send 'em DHL and get 'em there next day," he offers.

"Nope. Draws too much attention on the receiving end, and it makes whatever it is look valuable. I don't want some asshole to take it off a porch or some shit like that before my guy gets it," I

104

explain. "So regular mail, first thing tomorrow, yeah?"

"Aye, aye, skipper. I get me some O.T. outta this? You ain't nothing but honky fuckin' trouble, know what I'm sayin'?" he grins.

"I do! That's why I'm bringin' yo black ass one mo'fuckin' souvenir when I get back, ya feel me?"

"I ain't feelin' you, gaywad! My ass only work one direction!" he jokes.

"Yeah, all five of'em at once! Harry's your favorite!" I won the Smack Talk Olympics with that dodgy bit of cleverness, which Tyrone graciously acknowledged.

"Homie damned sure better bring me somethin' good back." I nodded at him with a smile and he grabbed me in a dude hug. "Keep it safe, whitey. Don't make me have ta fuck you up!" Tyrone warns.

"Word."

"Go play army wit'cher boys. I see ya when ya back in the cracker hood."

"Thanks, man," I say. "And thanks again for the great job on the props."

"Ain't nothin' but a thang!" Tyrone says, and disappears into the building. It was officially for real. Operation Dutch Oven had begun.

Chapter 6

THE REST AREA WAS fairly deserted, save

for the older couple in their lime green and rust caravan, and a family of religious folk of some sort. They were dressed like they were from Little House on the Prairie. We stopped a bit further up the parking area and piled out of our nifty van.

"All right, lads, it's time for our transport briefing. Our Mr. Johnnie, here, is gonna tell us how we're gettin' where we're goin'. So pay him some mind!" Captain Lanning announced. The guys formed a semi-circle around me as I sat down on the top of a picnic table.

"Thanks, Captain," I began. "So my job is to get you where you need to be, transport you during your mission, and then get you back to Denmark safe and sound," I explained. "The first one is easy. The second one *should* be. But it's that third one that's the bitch. A lot of it depends on how well the mission goes, but knowing what I've heard of you all, I don't expect that to be an issue."

"You got that bloody right, mate," joked one of the SAS team.

"Give the lads a quick primer on tomorrow," Lanning said. "I think we'd all like to know what to expect."

"Awesome," I began. "So this is the plan. We have two safe houses we'll be taking advantage of on the way to Ukraine. One's a couple hours this side of Warsaw. The other is fifteen kilometers before we hit the Ukrainian border at Medyka. We'll be at the first one tonight."

"So it'll be two days before we get there?" Lanning asked.

"Yes, and there's a reason for that. First, it's a hellacious border to cross. Sometimes it can take up to a whole day before they'll let you in. Depends on the mood of the guy in charge that day. You should be rested. Leaving Poland will be easy enough. It's when we get to the entry point—a place called Shehyni—that it gets dodgy," I explained. "So I want to get you to the border after a good night's sleep." Then I told them about my insurance policy.

It wasn't exactly Standard Operating Procedure, and I hadn't mentioned it at my initial briefing when the insertion plan got approved. But I knew that if we played the American hubris card, and assumed that everyone wearing a Ukrainian border guard uniform was a mindless idiot, then we would deserve it if the plan failed.

Yes, I know we can be clever. But so can they. And believe it or not, despite the stereotype that anyone of Russian—or in this case, Ukrainian— heritage is a lazy and disinterested worker, the folly will be ours if we're sloppy.

"So what's changed?" the Dutch major asked.

"On the day we cross the border there will be another van. I'll take a few of you guys with me, and the major or the captain will drive the rest in *this* van," I explained, indicating the vehicle we'd been driving. "The reason for that is to get a time stamp on the oil company van. They will log the van in when we cross, and they will log it out when we leave."

"I don't quite understand," the major said.

"When we enter Ukraine with both vans, they will show different number plates. Our work vehicle for your job will be the second van. The first one will head straight for Romania just as the transfer visa says. And it will cross *into* Romania, clearing out the transfer visa. In effect, you now have as much time as you need to do the deed, and the authorities, if they pull the border records looking for any foreign vehicles that may have played a part in the mission, will discard any suspicions about the oil worker van. As far as they'll know, you drove straight to Romania and left Ukraine in your rear view mirror."

"Wow. So who's driving the van to Romania?" Lanning asked.

"Some local hires I've worked with before. They're actually Romanian gypsies and they do this kind of work brilliantly. Just don't hire them to fix your roof or add on to your house. This'll give you the time you need to assess the local temperature for getting your job done as cleanly as you can. It'll work," I promised.

"Let's hear it for Johnnie, lads!" Lanning laughed. We took another half hour to enjoy the break and then saddled up and hit the road.

We got to our first safe house at seven o'clock, and the crew was ready for a hot shower and a good meal. Ironically, it was the old Black Site that Sander and I had stayed at with the fake CIA asset we were delivering on my very first assignment.

We drove past the little lake where he told me what he'd overheard; that the guy was really a Russian who had somehow gotten rid of the real asset and was poised to do some kind of harmful business. It seemed so long ago. And yet I was here again and the sight of the lake, the cute little cabins and out buildings, and the big barn (that was obviously where the many CIA detainees were "questioned") served as the focal point for the now defunct base. I missed my man.

After everyone was down for the night I pulled my cot over to the fireplace hearth. The glow of the fire and the flickering flames painted light against the walls and off the ceiling. It was like a show from a child's paraffin Magic Lantern from a century ago. Slides of amazing wonders of the world, kings, queens, royal dancing steeds, and great sailing ships would hypnotize the young dreamers as they hoped these wondrous sights would someday be theirs to claim.

My wondrous sight was six hundred miles away in a Danish thatched roof farmhouse, and I missed him. I thought how much he would enjoy lying next to me, his fingers gently rubbing my back while we softly talked of our day.

Long Before Morning

I felt a tear welling up in my right eye. How can a person miss another so damned much? At quiet, reflective times like this it was difficult to be alone. I wanted to feel him next to me, and feel his breath against my neck. I would have rolled to face him and would have kissed him. I would have kissed his chest, his cheek, his forehead. And I would have kissed his lips.

A stirring appeared and I instinctively reached into my underwear and held my dick. It was hard. Then I rubbed my balls and began squeezing the base of my cock. It was useless to try and ignore what I knew was going to happen, so I yanked off my shorts and laid down on my back.

It started slowly at first. Just gentle, long strokes as lightly as I could make them. I pressed on the underside surrounding my head, and then steadily increased the stroking until the peaceful bliss of stimulation and imagination collided and headed for a boil.

I saw us on the bed at the Nyhavn 71 Hotel that very first night we made love. I saw Sander without a stitch of clothing lying face down on our huge bed, just waiting for me to massage his gorgeous form from head to toe.

His lovely scent pervaded my fantasy as my fist furiously pumped on my angry cock. I could see the back of his neck and I knew I was inside him, the feeling building so intensely while he clamped his butt cheeks against the outward thrusts of my engorged penis. These were the fantastic thoughts my mind conjured as I neared the powerful orgasm I was generating.

I breathed heavily now. My thighs were straight and tense as lumber, and my toes were curling. The head was so sensitive and I was past the point of no return.

When my butt cheeks involuntarily clenched, and my nuts slapped around like racquet balls, I knew my critters were about to launch. And there they were! *Aagghh!* Oh God, what a glorious feeling! Praise Jesus! Oh, yeah! *Aaahhh... Fuck!* The most wonderful feeling in the world! It just kept cumming! Damn! Oh shit! No cum rags. I didn't plan for cum rags! God damn it! Oh well, guess I'll just lie here in my spooge for awhile. Hey, maybe the fire can dry it out. That's dumb. Sorry, Mr. Undershorts. You're being pressed into duty. I don't wanna hear another word about it. God, us guys are gross! I *love* it. Yep. I do.

113

Chapter 7

UKRAINE

Eugeny BEGAN HIS DAY LIKE MANY

others before this one. He was totally and completely pissed off. Five people owed him money, and that fucking wop, Claudio, had worn his patience down to his last Ukrainian nerve. He hadn't seen Claudio since they helped down the big jet the year before. At least the Kremlin paid their fucking debt for that one. That was the only thing that had kept his sanity.

His girlfriend was turning out to be a real cow, and when he learned that Claudio was borrowing her for his own immoral purposes (behind his back, no less), well, that was the break for him. If he wanted to fuck her, all he would have had to do was ask. There are protocols for this kind of thing. But no, Claudio had to be the sneaky Italian bitch that he is and try and play Valentino to anyone he fancied. Even to a sloppy Uke chick from Kiev. She was *his* sloppy Uke, though, and Eugeny wasn't about to be cuckolded by that kinky-haired, unshaven piece of Neapolitan asshole. Fuck him!

Then he was paid a visit from, of all people, the tax authorities. It seems that even a career criminal like him wasn't impervious to the long arm of the state treasury. Hell, they didn't care how you earned your money as long as you paid tribute to Caesar. What a fucking mess. So now he had to shake some trees of his own just to scratch the money together that he would only end up turning over to the government. But he knew he had to do it or else risk another kind of shakedown entirely.

Had he lost his touch? Shit, he was only twenty-four, but he was wondering if he had peaked. There was a time, not that long ago, when the very idea of anyone owing him so much as a kopek was as foreign to him as that fuck, Claudio. And to have *five* different parties owing him at the same time? He'd definitely lost the plot. A self-doubting criminal is not a good criminal to be.

"Rezlan, it is Eugeny, you fucker! Answer your phone, asshole, or deal with the consequence! I want my fucking money!" was what he barked into his mobile phone. Change up the name four more times, and that's how he spent his morning. *I probably should have sent out a group text,* he thought, berating himself for having let this go on for as long as it had.

The only thing he could really do was wait for someone to call him back. He swore that once he'd collected what was owed him, he'd never let things get this way ever again. In fact, he thought, some kind of holiday or getaway was long overdue. All work and no play makes Eugeny a very dull boy indeed.

Long Before Morning

IT HAD BEEN A LITTLE OVER A YEAR since the big day in the eastern fields of Donetsk Oblast. The Airplane Day.

The Butcher had known of a group of Pro-Russian rebels who were committed to using any means necessary to defeat the Ukrainian government's arrogant assumption that they were their own nation. Ukraine was and always shall be a protectorate and part of whatever prevailing Russian state is at any given time, they thought. History supports this, the rebels claimed, and so they formed their own separatist militias to drive the point home by force. Of course it helped that the Kremlin provided support for their cause in every way, shape, and form. So The Butcher got tapped to help put a job together for the political miscreants— nothing more than bullies, really. They just liked fighting.

The insurgency was gaining a little more ground every day, and the West's aversion to anything other than throwing token amounts of money at their sworn enemy was definitely helping their growth and success. None of them—the Americans, French, Germans, the Brits—*none of them* would ever commit a single soldier to fight against them, this they knew. And so they hunkered in to take full advantage of it.

Sure, let them fill the Ukrainian government bank accounts with Western guilt money. None of it will get to their tin soldier army anyway. It'll just get shuffled into deep political pockets, never to be seen again. (Unless you suddenly notice some new dachas popping up in some pricey places far from the conflict in, oh, say a year to eighteen months.)

Eugeny was picked by The Butcher to drive some "borrowed" ammo for a Buk SAM missile system all the way across the country, and then to help with whatever needs doing once he'd arrived. Thing is, it wasn't an easy job at all. He was supposed to acquire a set of four missiles, drive them straight-faced across a country mired deeply in political flux—many of the roads treacherously outdated and in massive disrepair—and deliver them to the Russian colonel in charge. This he had to do on time and with a smile. One tiny detail: The missiles are about the length of a pickup truck and each weigh about a quarter of a ton.

"How am I to get twenty-eight-hundred kilos of missiles to Eastern Ukraine, asshole?" Eugeny had said that day to The Butcher. "Besides, since when do I becomes beeg arms dealer?"

"You become what we say you become!" The Butcher shouted into the phone. "You will meet your

Italian friend where we told you, and you will make your plan and see it through. He has an engine block hoist, and two long-bed vans. You want me to teach you to drive, too, shithead?" The Butcher scolded.

"What's the pay?" Eugeny asked.

"Whatever you get paid. Now get to work!"

The call went dead, much as he would be if he screwed this up. He shifted into challenge mode. He would see it through, get paid, and consider future options. Now it was off to Claudio's junk yard and wherever this week would take him.

"FUCK THIS! IT WON'T WORK! STOP!" Claudio yelled. "When they left them here they had a fork lift!"

"You want to be the one who says we're not coming?" Eugeny challenged. "It will not be me, that's for sure. So let's figure it out, you wop bastard!"

"Fuck your mother with my FIAT!"

"It's too hot for this shit from you! Get your hairy ass behind that engine block lift and crank it up!" Eugeny shouted.

"It won't work!"

"Let me see that!" Eugeny bounded under the heavy duty 'saw horses' where the missiles lie, and approached the lift. It took him exactly three seconds to spot the problem. "Hey, idiot!" he began. "Do you see this?"

"What?"

"This little metal cotter pin that is right in front of your fat nose!"

"Cotter pin?"

"Yes. Cotter pin." Eugeny slowly exhaled, relieved that he'd solved the problem. Disgusted that Claudio was such a dumbfuck.

"What is it for?"

"To keep idiots like you getting your mental welfare from the fucking government, that's what!" Eugeny loosened the large nut and removed the pin. "There, genius. Now try it." The ease of which the first missile lifted off the cradle surprised even Eugeny. Once hanging, it was easy enough to guide the missile into the van, and then lower it onto the blocks that Claudio had fashioned for the trip. Say what you will about Claudio, the man was a fantastic metalworker.

An hour later and they were ready to go. With a few tins of beans, some cold pasta, and a stack of spread sandwiches, the two headed east, each behind the wheel of a non-descript van. They were on the clock.

---

17 JULY 2014—"WHERE ARE WE TO meet him?" Claudio asked Eugeny. The two were leaning against the back of the second van, eyes trained on the road next to the petrol station they were parked at.

"Here. That's all I know," Eugeny replied.

"Yesterday it is too warm. Today it looks like rain."

"Really, Claudio? You talk of the weather? God, how do your countrymen survive?" Eugeny sneered.

"Better than yours, it seems. At least the food's good in Italy, and we have Rome. You have shit."

"I would argue with you if I could," Eugeny said, shrugging his shoulders. "Enjoy this moment because it is seldom you say anything right."

"Look there!" Claudio exclaimed. "My God, what is it?"

"I think it's our ride."

A large, flat vehicle crawled slowly towards them, a futuristic machine set delicately upon it. Like something out of *Star Wars*. A serious looking man in Russian fatigues stuck his head out of the cab. The vehicle stopped beside the vans, blocking the entrance to the petrol station.

"Waiting for me?" the short-haired man with the cop mustache asked the two confused young men standing on the well-worn asphalt. "I am Strelkov. You may call me Strelkov," the now-retired Russian military intelligence colonel stated. Over the whole of his career, the man had expressed political viewpoints and actions that made Richard Nixon look like a bleeding heart liberal. And now he'd tossed his hat in with the separatist movement that would like nothing more than to see Russia revert to the old Soviet days.

He believed in Empire and Imperialism, as long as he found himself at the top of the pig trough, slopping with the other party big shots. One thing that the military academy had taught him was that there is no party, or party heads, unless the might of the sword stands behind them. His particular niche he'd carved was to make sure that anyone who could keep him in favor recognized that without him, they were nothing.

His latest gambit was to do anything he could to destabilize Ukraine so that Mother Russia could step in and reclaim what was rightfully hers. Ukraine should be a Russian province, he believed, not a sovereign state.

"Fall in behind me. We go for perhaps fifteen kilometers, and then enter on a farm road. I'll drive slow," Strelkov quipped. "Keep an eye on me! Don't lose me!"

"THAT WAS THE LONGEST DAMNED hour I have ever spent," Eugeny complained, hopping out of the van after backing it up to the SAM launcher. "I think you drew the short straw with this posting, Strelkov."

The career colonel smirked at the ignorant bastard, and just shook his head as he guided the second van into position. Offloading the missiles onto the launch platform went surprisingly fast. Arming them was a semi-automatic process that required some codes and some visual checks, but by mid-morning they were ready to fire.

"So now what?" Claudio asked.

"We wait. The Ukes are sending a plane to knock my comrades into next week, but this will not happen,"

"Oh?" Eugeny said.

"Yes. We will get word that it is headed this way and then bang! No more Ukes in the skies. At least not today," Strelkov boasted.

"Amazing," Claudio beamed. "How do you make them go?"

"What?"

"The bombs! How do they know where to go?"

"You push that big button there," Strelkov said, indicating the launch panel, "and then the missile.....it knows what to do."

"Stop being a pest, Claudio," Eugeny warned.

"It's okay. I used to be curious long ago," Strelkov admitted.

"Are you no longer curious?" Claudio asked. Strelkov shook his head.

"My boy, once you have seen everything, curiosity falls away. And I've seen it all," Strelkov replied.

Eugeny went for a smoke, surveying the endless farmland surrounding him. Strelkov cautioned him about extinguishing his cigarette before discarding it. It was obvious why—it was the height of summer and the grass and discarded wheat husks made for some great kindling. Still, Eugeny found it comical that Strelkov would concern himself with such a trivial matter when his war toy would no doubt expend magnificent fireballs upon releasing its payload into the stratosphere. It didn't take a rocket scientist, Eugeny thought.

---

17 JULY 2014—1500 HOURS (3 p.m.) LOCAL TIME. The Little Dutch Boy is what his family's friends had called him ever since he could remember, and his best mate, Joost, made sure that all the kids on his football team knew it too. It was funny, because Gary was one of the most stockiest and well-built young men on the team. He'd stopped being the Little Dutch Boy by the time he turned twelve. Age fifteen now, Gary excels at football, and is a very well-loved goal keeper—though his friends don't love him because he's a great goalie. They love him for his sense of humor, and his ready-to-go-at-all-times attitude that ensures he'll never miss anything in life.

Come by Gary's house at eight o'clock on a Saturday night saying that you want to build an igloo farm behind the Zuiderzee Dyke and sell air conditioners, and he'll be the first to grab his coat shouting *Be back soon, Mom!* as the screen door slams behind him.

This day found young Gary on another adventure. He was at ten thousand meters, high above the clouds, winging his way to, of all places, Malaysia. On holiday with his mom, he was so excited that he could barely contain himself. In the three hours since boarding the mighty Boeing Triple-Seven airliner, he'd taken a gob of selfies, had about five soft drinks, a snack, and they'd just finished a fantastic lunch. Well, he had to admit he really didn't care for whatever it was — his tastes were more of the meat and potatoes variety. But it sure looked fancy, and it smelled real good.

Gary had also made friends with the young Indonesian boy sitting to his left, and the two were planning a video game challenge on his phone once lunch was completely cleared away, and the others began watching movies and stuff.

Mom Petra was engrossed in a magazine, and Gary thought his row was special because the trays came up from the sides of the chairs, not from the seatbacks in front of you like everyone else's. That was because their row was up against the bulkhead, and because of that there was more legroom. He sorely needed that, and breathed a sigh of relief when he first saw their seats once they boarded.

"Where do you live, anyways?" Gary asked the boy, Ezekiel.

"Near Amsterdam," he replied in nearly native Dutch. "I'm going to see my dad," he explained. "He works for Shell in Surabaya."

"Really? My mom used to work for them. Cool," Gary said. "What games do you got...?" and on it went from there. They were two kids who hadn't known each other when they woke that morning, but were now comparing notes on all that matters within their burgeoning worlds. They had more in common, than not.

"YES! YES! I COPY! WE'VE GOT THEM!" Strelkov barked with glee into the radio. He followed the incoming AN-26 Ukrainian war bird. No telling what the bastards planned to do with it, he thought. An AN-26 can be used for all kinds of mischief, even bombing. He surmised that they were bringing in reinforcements. The fuckers might even parachute in

128

and start jamming monkey wrenches into their plans by day's end. Not if he could help it.

"Hey, boys. Look at this!" he told Eugeny and Claudio. "These Ukes must think we're brain dead! Look!"

The two saw the blip on the radar screen and were clearly fascinated by it. Claudio was hypnotized. "Is that the airplane?" he asked.

"The very one. And we're gonna stop it in its hairy little tracks!" Strelkov announced.

"Wow! How do we do it?"

"In a couple minutes this button will be pressed and then we'll be finished with that particular bit of housekeeping," Strelkov bragged.

"Housekeeping?" Claudio asked.

"The airplane will go boom!" Eugeny said. "You dumbfuck!"

---

17 JULY 2014 — 1518 HOURS (3:18 p.m.) LOCAL TIME.
"I think Robert Downey Jr. is so fucking cool, man! *Iron Man* is the best movie ever," Gary insisted, as Ezekiel continued his round of play on the device.

"Don't say that," Petra scolded. "He's younger than you."

"What?"

"You know what!" Petra smiled. "Watch your language."

"I haven't even seen *Iron Man 3* yet. But I'm gonna get it off Amazon when we get back home," Gary continued.

"We saw it," Ezekiel added, "and I just got it off the Torrent."

"My friend does that, but my mom won't let me cause she's convinced the--"

Oh, God! The noise! He bit deep into his tongue and he saw the slight form of Ezekiel flying away, then he was over him. The sky is very blue, but it's so fucking cold! *I'm holding Mom's hand*, he thought for an instant. *No. The wind keeps my hand against me! A football slammed into my face! No, that happened three weeks ago in Maassluis. What the hell?!* The Little Dutch Boy falls to earth.

Black. Everything is black.

It is 17 July 2014 at 1520:36 Local Time.

Chapter 8

PARKOUR
Present Day

JOHNNIE HAD BEEN AWAY FOR THREE

excruciating days now. *It's always the same,* Sander thought. The first couple of days are the worst because imaginations tend to run wild. Sander knew from his own experience that time he rode along on Johnnie's first solo assignment and wound up with a bullet wound in his arm. This meant that Johnnie could never paint him a rosy picture of his work time spent away from home. Sander knew better.

He was pleased that at least this time he'd be extra busy. Sander was the star Free Runner on his Parkour team. Parkour had really become something since first attracting world consciousness through the fantastic opening scene of the James Bond movie, *Casino Royale.*

Sander Hansen had become quite the Parkour Pro since joining Team Dannebrog a couple years before. Now he was team captain, and was designing the lion's share of the challenges. And like anything cutting edge, the sport went from one of scrappy urban thumb-in-the-eye-of-authority, to corporate respectability. Now there were sponsors, and tickets were being sold. But for all of that, Sander only did it for one reason—pure joy.

The feeling he got from suddenly blasting off into a full run and jumping six feet high to land against a brick building, with a rusted drainpipe as his only means of ascension, was boner inducing.

He first attempted it on a dare when his friend, Anders Nielsen, bet him that he couldn't run from the top of one building to another at the Korup Skole. Not only did he do it (three times!), he loved it. He was hooked. And that November, when *Casino Royale* appeared at the Rosengård Cinemas, well, it was a done deal. He was Parkour Pokey from that moment forward.

Sander's phone went off. He didn't recognize the number. Johnnie, maybe? "Yes, it's Sander."

"Hey, man, what's up?" the voice said.

"Who is it?" Sander asked. He didn't know the voice.

"It's Per. From school."

"Per?"

"Per Larsen. We had art, sport, and history--"

"--Yes, Per. I remember you, of course. Why are you calling me?" Sander was totally confused by this. If he didn't know better, he'd think he was being punked by somebody. "I mean--"

"Yeah. Well, I wanted to say how cool I think you are because I saw you two weeks ago in Roskilde," Per said. "I mean it. You were awesome!"

"You were at the meet, then?" Sander asked.

"It was unbelievable! Where the hell did you learn to do that shit, man?" Per wondered, genuinely amazed. "I saw that one guy who said that we could try out for it if we wanted and, well, I want to."

"Ah! Yes, well, okay. You just have to come to practice and then sign up and all that. They'll—I mean, we'll give you all the info then."

Sander told him the when and the where, and then ended the call feeling very confused. Per had just talked to him like they were best mates. But in the entire time he knew him, from Klasse 4 until leaving school, Per was a monster. He never once said anything nice to Sander. He took every

133

opportunity to subtly put him down and make him feel less-than. He was a clever bully; the kind who never gets caught. In fact, he was a teachers' favorite. He came from a very nice family, and his parents were very active in all of the school activities, overnights, and sports. Oh, and one other thing— Sander had a massive, ongoing crush on Per Larsen since the day he met him back when they were nine years old.

Sander had pined over Per forever, and when puberty hit it was torturous. If he could gather up all the cum he'd spilled jacking off over the thoughts he'd had of Per Larsen, there would be enough to double the population of India. Probably China, too.

It really hurt when they were about twelve and the typical homophobic insults and slurs made the rounds throughout the halls and classrooms. The kid leading the chorus of faggot jokes and putdowns? Why a one Per Larsen, of course. And was he ever good at it. Some of them were kind of clever and even funny, Sander had to admit. But he didn't laugh. And when Sander was outed by his former boyfriend that day in the cafeteria, Per seized upon *that* gift like a late night T.V. talk show after a Republican senator gets caught swallowing a load in a public toilet. And now he'd just taken a phone call from the bastard of those countless hours of bullying, and the guy had acted like it was Old Home Day. What the fuck? I guess it's true, what they say about success being the best revenge, he thought. Maybe the asshole would forget to show up and he could once again forget all about all of it. Especially the phone call.

PARKOUR PRACTICE IS ONE OF Sander's favorite things to attend on earth. He gets up earlier than he has to. He rearranges his kit bag at least three times before heading out the door. And he's always the first one there, and the last to leave. When he pulled into the gravel covered car park there was a little white Peugeot over on the grass, and the driver had reclined the seat for a nap.

"Hey! Wake up!" Sander said, tapping on the driver's side window. "Come help me set up." It was Per. He shot up and was happy to see that it was Sander who had found him asleep in the car.

"Hey, man! Good to see you. It didn't take as long as I thought it would to get here from Korsør," Per said.

135

"Is that where you live now?" Sander asked.

"Yeah. We moved there a year after Sofus finished school." Sofus is Per's younger brother, and ironically was always very kind to Sander. How those two could have come from the same household was anybody's guess. "So what do we do to get ready?" Per asked.

"See those pallets, barrels, the outdoor furniture, and those big crates?" Sander indicated. "Well those were left that way after our last practice. Now we change them all around, close those windows there, and open that big sliding door. We just have to make a new mess, but not too easy of one," he said.

Parkour is the art of Free Running. The participants climb the sides of buildings, leap between rooftops, slither down drainpipes, and even skinny up to the tops of flagpoles or radio towers all with whatever is available to help them achieve their goals. If a stack of boxes happens to be adjacent to a building, and those boxes are placed in a way that the Free Runner can jump from the top of the pile and land on another building that leads to another potential landing spot, and do this against a very tight clock, the Parkour runner is graded highly by his peers.

On the other hand, Free Runners can die from missteps and falls, or at the very least find themselves paralyzed from injuries sustained during a match. Some days a broken arm or a severely sprained ankle is considered getting off easy.

"Who decides the course," Per asked.

"Me."

"Cool. So is there a beginner training I can do? I really haven't done anything like this," Per said. "I don't wanna get in anybody's way, but I really want to do something."

"No worries," Sander said. "We breakout into groups first, and I'll work with you because you're new."

"Then I buy beers after, okay? To say thanks!"

"Sure. Yeah, sounds good."

The team gathered within the hour and the clubhouse part of the meeting was handled. Dues were paid, and the new recruits, including Per, were introduced. Ninety percent of the newbies would never come back once they'd had a go at a base run. And the first knee and elbow scrapes were usually enough to put the dabblers off. But at least they could tell their friends they'd tried it.

Sander had the feeling that Per would be a keeper. He always excelled at everything he tried in school, and there was never a team, group, or club that he wasn't captain of back in those days. And he was certainly physically fit.

Speaking of which, Sander couldn't help but notice Per's fine form once he'd changed into his running gear. The shortest shorts. No underwear; he was free-balling it. His white t-shirt betrayed the weight training that Per had never waivered from. And his legs; well, they were strong as oxen, and his thighs were perfection defined. And when he turned and bent over to rub and warm up said perfect legs, the gorgeous ass Sander had spent years admiring was there before him, bathed in perfect light.

"Sander! Stop looking at your friend's ass! What will Johnnie say?!" shouted Carsten, the team secretary and treasurer. "Put your eyes back where they belong!" he laughed. Of course everybody on the team knew Sander was gay, and most times Johnnie would tag along to help set things up and be the water boy. So nothing was secret.

"Fuck off, Carsten!" Sander joked. "I'm a happily married man!"

"Just keepin' you honest, my boy!" was Carsten's retort. "Less butt-looking, and more Free Running!"

Per's ears perked up and as he turned around to

face Sander, *Here it comes,* Sander thought. Why should anything be different now?

"So, you're still gay! It wasn't just a phase, I see," Per smiled.

"Yeah. Still gay."

"That's good," Per said.

"Why? So you can fuck with me? Well, we're grown-ups now, right? So it won't work."

"What won't?"

"You giving me shit for being who I am. It worked when we were kids in school, but not anymore," Sander declared.

"I'M SORRY IF I MISUNDERSTOOD what you were getting at," Sander told Per. They went to a coffee bar in Fredericia at Per's urging so he could set a few things straight. "It's just that you were never that nice to me before, especially when Torben outed me that day at school."

"I was a complete asshole, Sander. It was wrong, and I'm really sorry about it," Per said. Sander nodded his acceptance and took a long sip of the Danish Blend coffee and followed it with a bite of

139

buttered scone. Maybe Per was legit, he thought. Stranger things had happened.

"Glad to see you've grown out of your mean streak," Sander quipped. "I always thought you should be more like your brother."

"I know. And there's something else I need to say, too."

"What is it?"

"Well, see, it's like this," Per began. "I don't know how to say it but just to say it." Sander was at the very least intrigued by the turn the conversation took. He shot Per a quick shrug. Per continued. "Uhmm, you know I had about a dozen girlfriends, right?"

"Yeah," Sander grinned, "and that was in klasse nine alone!" Per chuckled and looked away, as if he didn't want to see Sander's reaction to what came next.

"See, thing is, Sander, the girls don't cut it for me. And when I saw you and your guy at the meet, something struck me. It struck me pretty hard," Per said.

"What?"

"How happy and comfortable you were with each other. I saw him kiss you and hug you when you made that killer score, and it just seemed so... It

140

just seemed natural. It seemed right, you know?" Per explained.

"That's cause it is right," Sander added. "And it's natural for us, anyway."

"That's what I mean! And I want that," Per said.

"With a guy?" Sander asked. "Really?"

"Really. So one of the... Part of the reason I called you is that... Sander, I don't know what I'm doing. I don't know the first thing about any of it."

"Any of what?"

"Sex!" Per said, his voice lowered to nearly a whisper.

"Bullshit, man! You're the sex machine of both Korup Skole and Marie Jørgensen's, too! Don't give me that," Sander said with a chuckle,

"I've never been with a guy, man. And it's driving me crazy. I think about it all the time, and I needed to ask what I do next," Per pleaded. "I'm lost, man!"

"I don't know. A porno, maybe? I mean, it's just basically what you've always done. I mean, what do you expect really? You stick things where they go," Sander said.

"I know, I know. I just want to do it right. I want to know what it's like before... Well, what if I'm crappy at it?"

141

"It's not so hard, really," Sander explained, "and you shouldn't have any trouble at all finding someone to be with you."

"Shit! That's what you think," Per complained.

"What? You're full of it! Hell, I'd have given anything to--"

"Teach me, Sander."

"What the--"

"Please. I trust you. Let me try it with you. I want you to be my first. No complications. No problems. I just need somebody I can trust who will show me what to do," Per told him.

"I'm... Per, I'm..."

"Married! I know. That's why it's perfect, because I know the situation. I know you're not gonna expect anything from me, either. We'll just mess around like mates do, and I'll know what it's like, and then I'll take what I learn from you and live my life like I should've been since we were in school," Per said.

"Wow. You've thought about this," Sander declared. "You really have."

"It's all I've thought about since I saw you at the meet. Since I saw you kiss your guy. I want that, Sander. I want it so bad, and I trust you. I do. You were always better than me, and I admit it," Per said.

"Better? What's that supposed to mean? Sorry, you lost me there."

"Why do you think I was such a fucking asshole to you all those years? You're better than me, Sander. You are the nice guy. You're the sweet guy that everybody just likes and trusts from the second they see you. You have compassion, and you aren't afraid to show it. You've always been like that, and I treated you like shit because of it. The whole school's always been jealous of you, don't you get it, man?" Per explained. "And so I'm admitting that, hoping that you'll have something in that heart of yours for me. I'm gay, Sander. Always have been, but I've just lived a lie until now, and it's time I be me. But I'm scared."

"I don't think that can ever happen," Sander said. "I mean, what you want to happen can't happen with me. I love Johnnie."

Per was visibly disappointed. He patted Sander on the thigh and told him he understood, thanking him for listening. "Crap. This is awkward now. I thought, or guess I assumed that gay guys never say no and are always ready for a shag," Per said. "I'm sorry I thought that."

"No, it's okay," Sander reassured him. "I used to crush on you all through school, and I understand about the stereotype. I guess Johnnie and me are

143

different about stuff like that than most guys are. But, yeah, thanks for thinking of me, I guess. No problem." And with that the meeting came to a close. Each went to their cars talking of mundane Parkour plans and next week's practice schedule.

Sander sat in his car and watched Per pull out of the drive and enter the highway. He had just caught a glimpse of the back of Per's thigh when he slid into the driver's seat of his car. Per was just as gorgeous as he's always been, and today he had asked Sander for sex. Oh, how the worm has turned, he thought.

Chapter 9

Border towns, no matter what part of the world you're in, are teeming with dodgy characters, corruption, and graft. Graft is the official currency. It was no different—in fact it was worse in some ways—at the Polish border with Ukraine.

We'd hit the deck early and filled up on what would likely be our last good meal for the foreseeable future, and drove in the opposite direction to a field that used to be a railway switching yard. Built by the Nazis, it was where the railway vans that moved the Jews to the extermination camps were stored and maintained.

"Men, if I could have your attention for a minute?" I said once we'd parked and left the van. "A few things, and these are really important, so pay attention. First, how many of you smoke?" I asked. "I know you do, Ron. And you, Garrett. Any Dutch or Aussies light up?"

"Well, yes. Just not ciggies," joked Malcolm from Perth.

"Nope. Just tobacco is all I need to know at the moment," I smiled. A total of five raised their hands and I could tell they didn't quite get what I was going for. Fair enough. "Right. So here's the deal," I continued. "If you have any brand cigarettes like Marlboros, Camels, Prince, Lark—any of those. Especially with filters. You need to smoke 'em up real quick and give whatever's left to me."

"Damn! They're dear, mate! Do we get 'em back?" asked one British soldier.

"Afraid not. But, no worries! I have here packs of crappy Eastern European brands, and some tobacco pouches, and even some papers! Yay, smokes! I'll trade ya!" I laughed, trying to make the best of the situation. Fact was, every detail had to be considered, including the reality that hourly oil workers from countries sharing the Ukrainian border don't buy expensive Western smokes.

146

"You heard him, lads! Let's have every last fag," Captain Lanning ordered. "Our Johnnie's right. Skuzzy scum like you lot don't buy Dunhill's."

Good natured moans and complaints followed, but the boys tossed their stash into the garbage bag I held open.

"I'll leave it to the captain and the major as to how they want to divide you up for the crossing. Once we get to the meeting point in Kiev we'll change you out for our Gypsy actors, and we'll all get back together and head for the hideout," I explained.

"A hideout and everything, lads! D'ya hear? We've a hideout!" Lanning kidded.

"Damned straight we do!" I chuckled.

"Will there be girls at the hideout?" one of the team shouted out. "And beer?"

"Nope!" I continued. "But if you're really good I'll let you listen to my Susan Boyle collection and we can play endless games of pub trivia."

"Bloody Yank!"

"What a right load o' pish!"

"Johnnie's a wanker!"

"Now, now, fellas! It's for your own good," I laughed. "Oh, look! Saved by the Romanians!" I pointed at the van pulling into the field. "Gentlemen, your limousine!"

147

The rust-laden crap van pulled up and parked beside us, the sinewy form of my friend, Nestor, smiling from behind the wheel, not the least bit embarrassed by his semi-rotting teeth.

"Nestor! Good to see you, my friend!" I greeted the stout, odiferous man. "I see you got the van. How about the package I sent you?"

"Package? What package?" Nestor replied.

"Now's not the time, my Roma amigo!"

"Yessss... I got the package. Just as you said," he smiled. I wish he didn't smile so much. A dentist could put three of his kids through college just from getting hired on to work on Nestor's big mouth. The things I put up with to advance the cause of freedom in the world...I'll tell ya.

"Good. Let's fix up the van and make it all nice and oil-workery, and then blow this pop stand," I said.

"What means this pop stand?" Nestor asked.

"Nestor... Fix up the van!"

AN HOUR LATER AND WE had passed through the Polish exit border. We were now in the no-man's

148

land—about five kilometers—before crossing into the Ukrainian side. We rounded the corner of the beaten-up four-lane road and met a conga line of cars, their motors still as they waited. And waited. And waited. Which is what we'd be doing for the foreseeable future. Hurry up and wait; that's my motto.

"So now what?" Lanning asked, clearly knowing the answer to his mostly rhetorical question.

"We wait our turn, boys," I said. "Maybe a game of Slug Bug with Ladas and Skodas instead, or some I Spy with My Little Eye?"

"Like I spy a fucking yellow-haired yank who's too bloody smart-arsed for his own good?" Lanning chortled with sarcasm.

"Did I ever tell you that Manchester United is a right bunch of wankers?" I said. By the way, have I ever mentioned what it's like to have empty juice boxes and apple cores thrown at the back of your head? The mission-specific camaraderie was kicking in, and despite the hard reason we were there it was a welcome emotion and we needed that.

Three hours later, inching closer and closer to the checkpoint, it was our turn. Talk about an anti-climax.

"Hello. Where are you from?"
"Romania."

149

"Where do you travel today?"

"Romania."

"Transit visa?"

"Yes. Please."

"One hundred kopeks."

"Here you go."

"One moment please."

"Yes."

"Here is your receipt and your transit visa. Give to official when you cross into Romania. Safe journey."

"Thank you. Good day."

And that was all there was to it. We were the greasy oil workers. Our passports said as much. No flags were raised. We were on our way. Next stop, Kiev.

Chapter 10

UNTHINKABLE

I HAVEN'T HEARD A THING FROM MY

Johnnie since he left. I'm lonely without him and my family does the best they can to keep me occupied, but we all know that's not the same thing.

It's going on five days now and he usually would have called me. He's sending me cute little things on Facebook, like favorite songs and such. But, yeah, it's not the same.

I love Jannik to pieces, but he gets underfoot sometimes. With him it's all about the timing. I won't have seen him for the entire day, and just when I want to have a little sleep or watch some bad television he pops in like a zoo monkey.

"Brother! Let's go to McDonald's!" "Pokey! Take your favorite brother to the gaming store!" "Hey, best friend! Let's ride bikes!"

What am I supposed to say to that? Of course we'll do whatever he wants because it's not his fault that his timing sucks. Or maybe he plans it that way. I don't know; I guess I'm just happy that he loves me enough to even want to hang out with me.

There goes the door. Now what?

"Hey!" It's Per. Parkour's not until tomorrow. Huh.

"Hey, Per. What's up?"

"I'm coming back from Esbjerg and Parkour's tomorrow. So I had an idea..."

"Yeah. Come in. It's just me and my brother. Johnnie's at work," I told him. We headed for the couch and plopped down. I asked him if he wanted something to drink and he mentioned a beer. "Watch this," I said. "HEY! JANNIK!"

"What?!" came the response from up in the loft.

"Come here!"

"Keep your pants on!" he hollered. "I'm on the way!" This was obvious from the earth shattering and ceiling-shaking thumps emitting from overhead. Why can't he just stand up, walk across the floor, and simply walk down the stairs like any other

152

humanoid bi-ped? Nope. It's always gotta be 8.1 on the Richter Scale.

"Where's the fire?!" he demanded. Then he saw Per. "Oh. Hi."

"Hey! I bet you're Jannik." Per smiled. Jannik nodded and looked my way.

"This is Per. He's on my team. And we would very much like some beers and snacks," I teased.

"Uh huh. What's in it for me?"

"Snacks," I replied.

"And beer," he countered, nodding his head with a wry smile plastered across his face.

"And no," I raised him. "Soda."

"Come on!"

"You can have a drink of mine. So get going."

"Asshole."

"That's what I put up with when Johnnie's away. Anyway, what's the big idea?" I asked Per.

"Oh, yeah. Well, you know it's an hour to Korsør, and I figured since I'm already coming from Esbjerg now, and just have to be back here again for practice... Well, would it be okay if I slept here on a couch or something so I can save all that time and gas?" he asked. Sure, I told him. No big deal at all. We were just going to ride into town for a pizza or some other crap food for dinner, so what's one more?

Long Before Morning

"Here's your snacks, oh slave master!" came Jannik's witty snark as he entered the room with his arms loaded to the gills. "So sorry your legs are broken," he added with sass.

"Piss off, you little creep! Be glad I have use for you, else you'd be outside with your fuzzy wolf pals," I chuckled. "Let's see what you got there."

"Good stuff! Only the good stuff!" he laughed. "And it's all for me."

"Wow! You guys are better than the tank station. They don't have shit this good!" Per enthused. "Damn!"

"Per's staying over, Spiderman. It's too far for him to go all the way to his house just to come back tomorrow," I explained.

"Are we still going to the town later?" Jannik wondered.

"Unless pizza knows how to walk here by itself, then the answer's yes."

"Good!" Jannik replied. "I can't do real food tonight. Must have junk."

"You're a cool little man," Per told Jannik. "Wish my brother and sister were as cool as you are." Per turned to me. "He's awesome."

"I know he is," I agreed, "but don't ever let him hear me say that."

"Um, hello Mister Stupid. I'm right here!" Jannik teased, waving his fingers in front of my face. He knows exactly what I think of him. He's always known that.

LOCATION: TIVOLI BASE CAMP, KIEV, UKRAINE

"THAT'S LAME, MATE! TIVOLI? SOUNDS a bit too much on the poofter side for me!" Lanning chuckled. For those who may not be as familiar with British slang and put-downery, a poofter is someone who is a male homosexual. Like me! You'll love where this bit of gay stereotyping comes from.

You see, according to macho English workingmen, the farts released from a gay guy's ass go "poof" instead of the loud, trumpet-like PHFFFTTTT! sound of a manly straight dude. That's because, according to Local Pub Scientific Fact, us gay boys have butt fucked so much that apparently our sphincters are too loose to produce that glorious elephant trumpeting.

"Well, Captain," I answered. "Perhaps you're right, because I'm a card carrying cocksucker and so

I'm prone to frilly things and silly names." I shot him a wink as I continued to set up my base camp café.

"Ah, go on! You're no queer lad! You're having me on! What you playin' at?! *Tivoli!* Hmmmph! What's a bloody Tivoli anyway?"

"It's an amusement park in Copenhagen. Cool rides. Okay food. Centrally located," I smiled. "Great place to pick up guys!" The look on his face was priceless.

"Hang on! Are you really...well, course you are. Nobody'd joke about that," Lanning said, "would they?"

"Dunno, Captain. But, yes, I'm one of *those!* Eighteen-thirty-hours good for mess?" I asked.

"Sorry?"

"To eat. Is eighteen-thirty-hours convenient for eating?"

"Oh, yes. Yes, of course," he replied, a bit dazed and preoccupied. Poor man. I'd crashed his world. "Wait! We have ORP's and such. Aren't they just going to eat when they want?"

"Well, they're happier when they get a served, sit-down hot meal, sir. I combine the rations, cook them, season them, serve 'em up on paper plates. Happy diners, happy soldiers!" I told him. "So . . ."

"Sorry?"

"Eighteen-thirty--"

"Yes! Yes, by all means. Eighteen-thirty-hours for dinner. Yes."

I think it's funny to see a bald dude scratch his head. He was definitely scratching his when I walked over to my cute little tent. Oh, us gays! We're just so... *Gay!*

"ARE WE NEVER GONNA HEAR nothing from Johnnie?" Jannik asked between big chomps of pineapple and Danish bacon pizza. We'd taken a trip into town for the pizza, and then planned to shunt to my parents' place so my brother could pick up some clothes and Legos. I keep meaning to have Johnnie buy stock in Lego so we can retire. That boy has more Legos than Legoland.

"You know how it works, Jan. He calls when he can," I said.

"What does he do, Sander?" Per asked.

"He works for the American government in Copenhagen."

"What's the American government do in Copenhagen?"

"They have business at their embassy, I think. It's something like that," I told him.

"He's a spy for the CIA," Jannik said casually, as he peered down at his phone.

"Yeah, sure!" Per laughed. "And I'm James Bond!"

"No, he is," Jannik said, deadpan. "And *he's* Pussy Galore," he continued, pointing at me. "But I understand if you don't believe me. It's Top Secret anyways."

Per was laughing uncontrollably, and could barely catch his breath. "I told you, Sander! That kid is so fucking cool!"

"Yeah," I smiled forcibly. "Real cool!" I shot Jannik a dirty look. "Real fucking cool!" Jannik just looked me square in the eye and performed his very unfair trick of raising each of his eyebrows separately, while sending me a huge smirk. I hate him! I laughed even bigger than Per.

THE LONG SUMMER NIGHT kept a magic-hour illumination glowing above Sander, Jannik, and Per as they drove the back roads from Odense to the pretty farming town of Gelsted. It is near this classic Danish village—once owned and administered by the Count and Countess of Aske-Gels—that the Hansen-Allen boys chose to make their home together. They pulled up the drive and Jannik beamed, excited when he spied his little wolf family waiting for him.

"Look who's here!" Jannik squealed. "Drop me! I'll walk the rest of the way with them!"

Sander stopped the car and Jannik bounded out, making a bee-line to the little wolf pack.

A while back he'd discovered a newborn wolf pup that had become stuck in the cobwire garden stake; it was a kind of protective fencing for the vegetable plot. Jannik had carefully approached the frightened pup. When he'd gotten to within a meter of the whining little ball of fur he was greeted by a very nervous, low-toned growl from its mother. At once he sat cross-legged on the ground and lowered his head to stare at his own lap.

"Mother worries about you," Jannik cooed. "But we need to get you free or you'll die."

He kept up his soothing patter, and as he felt with his hands the best way to release the pup, he slowly raised his head to make eye contact with the wolf mother to his right. Then he sat there for nearly

159

half an hour just petting the pup. Finally, when the mother seemed calmer, he quickly raised the fencing and pulled the pup out of harm's way.

The mother bolted upright and stiffened, so Jannik laid on his belly, gently stroking her pup. He lowered his head in a gesture of deference and waited as she cautiously moved toward him.

"Here's your baby. Come and see," Jannik purred at Mother Wolf. She responded. Moments later she was standing over the pup, then she bent down and began to lick the squirming form of her little wolf puppy.

Jannik opened his hands allowing the mother to pick him up with her mouth, and away she trotted. The following week he would learn that she had taken up residence behind the garden shed, and she and her little brood would stay there until they were old enough to either join or start a pack of their own.

That's when Jannik started spoiling them with hunks of hamburger and bowls of fresh water. He even named them. And now, like on this warmish evening, they eagerly looked forward to his return, because little human boy always equals big tasty hamburgers! That, and he saved her third born pup when he had decided to go exploring that day without her permission. She had named him Bright

One, inspired by the human who had returned him to her unharmed. Jannik called him Sparrow, because he'd fallen from the nest. And now they were friends.

"Wolves? That's fucking dangerous, man!" Per told Sander with concern.

"Yeah, you'd think so. But he rescued one of the mom's pups, and I guess she's totally okay with him. He feeds them sometimes, and he plays with them. She doesn't mind," Sander explained. "I told him if he goes missing and I find an extra smelly pile of wolf poop in the garden, I'll know what happened."

"Man! That's not funny!"

"Truly it's okay, Per. I'm just joking. He's even practically domesticated them, and the pups love him. The mom doesn't even pay attention to him anymore. In fact, the gamesman found out about it and told us that she looks at Jannik as one of her pups," Sander said.

"Wow! Then it's incredible. That's just way too cool."

Long Before Morning

IT HAD BEEN A VERY ENJOYABLE day, Sander thought. The trip into town. Jannik was in rare form, his sense of humor lightening the day to no end. Per had really turned out to be a good guy, and was going a long way to make the effort. He knew he had not been good to Sander when they were kids. He genuinely felt bad for it, too. Especially since he had recently come to terms with his own sexuality.

Imagine what it must be like to be the big man at school, the emerald of every girl's eye, and the admired sports hero of every other boy there. And be gay.

Everyone had their own opinion of Per Larsen; they had devised whatever scenario they believed about what his perfect life must be like. They had him marrying the perfect girl. They imagined him to be the sought after stud in a romance novel. The pop star. The sex engine. The football hero who sends his team to the World Cup.

But Per Larsen was none of those things, and deep inside he knew it. Hence the bullying. The borderline cruelty. The selfishness. And then one day it hit him square in the nose: Per Trune Larsen, you are a gay. You have always been gay, and you always knew it. When you were fucking all those girls, you would pretend they were boys.

Remember when Tina Rasmussen broke up with you and she told her friends that you always liked to do it from behind? That you never wanted to face her?

How about when you made Katrina Swanson cut her hair into a bob so she'd look exactly like a boy? You knew she had grown her hair her whole life, and that she loved her long hair. But she did it for you. She did it because she loved you. And you would only call her Kat because when you'd have sex, you'd pretend like it was a boy's name that you'd call out just before you came.

But you finally did admit to yourself who you are, albeit too late for saving a slew of broken hearts.

And then you saw Sander and Johnnie that afternoon at the Parkour event. You saw what love is. You saw two guys who are totally in love, and you wanted it. Badly. Fair enough, Per.

But why do you feel the need to seek it at the expense of people who don't see what your exact motivation for befriending them is?

"Hey, Sander?" Per whispered through the bedroom door. Johnnie and Sander's bedroom door.

"Yeah? Come in," Sander called. Per entered the room and softly shut the door behind him. "What's up?"

163

"I got a question for you, and I trust what you say about it," Per explained. "I need your advice on something."

"Yeah, sure," Sander replied from the bed. He was reading part of a novel he and Johnnie were sharing, and he wanted to get as many chapters ahead as he could so he could threaten to reveal spoilers. He would never do it, of course, but Johnnie was fun to tease.

He also would write little love notes on the pages for Johnnie to find. Or he'd write a completely random joke that had absolutely nothing to do with anything relevant to the book. And his favorite trick was to rip out a page every so often and replace it with a ransom note. The only way to pay the ransom and collect the missing page? A romp in the hay with his favorite gay!

"So, like I said the other day. I'm, uh, gay. And I don't have experience and so I wanted to ask you if you would take a look at me and tell me if I have what a guy is looking for," Per said.

"I don't get what you mean exactly," Sander replied.

"Can I get my clothes off and show you what I look like? And will you give me your complete honest opinion of if a guy will like me or not?"

164

"Well, I'm sure any guy will like you that way, Per. But it's more than that, you know."

"Yeah, I know that it's about personality and a bunch of other stuff. But if I go to a bar, or to a club, that's not what anybody thinks about. I want to know if--"

"--If you're Hot or Not?" Sander asked.

"Exactly! And I trust you."

This was awkward. Sander had wondered for years what lie beneath the stylish togs of Per Larsen. Here was his chance. Standing less than four feet away was the perfect body of the guy who'd starred in countless of his masturbatory fantasies, basically begging to disrobe in front of him. Things he had wondered for over a decade could be revealed with a simple... "Yes."

"Yeah? And you'll be honest with me?"

Sander nodded his head and felt his throat go dry. He tried to swallow, but only dryness responded. He cleared his throat and sat up, his back against the mahogany headboard. He caught a chill when he leaned against it, and quickly stuck a barrier pillow to ease the cold shock. Cold shock, indeed.

"Of course I'll be honest. Go ahead, then," Sander told him.

Per removed his shirt, and simultaneously

kicked off his shoes. He tossed the shirt on the foot of the bed, and then loosened his belt. A quick unsnapping above the zipper, and his trousers fell to the floor.

"I should have stripper music!" Per joked, as he untangled the jeans from around his ankles, then using his right foot to kick them away. Sander smiled at the lame stripper joke and realized that within seconds all of his childhood curiosity regarding Per Larsen would be forever put to rest. And then there it was. The most excellent example of physical male perfection anyone should have a right to possess.

The penis hung like a Michelangelo sculpture. It was larger than most, beautifully intact, as thankfully all Scandinavian men enjoy their penises without the mutilation of circumcision.

His balls were of equal size and peeked out to the left and the right of his member, and they hung low in their smooth sack.

There was a tuft of beautiful blond pubic hair, and the rest of his body was devoid of hair save for the armpits, with very little on his lower legs.

"Well?" Per asked.

"Uh, yeah . . . I think you're, uh . . ."

"What? Am I okay?"

"You're more than okay, Per. Seriously. You're--"

166

"--Hot?"

"Yes, Per. You're very hot. You have nothing to worry about. You'll be starting fights at the clubs," Sander told him.

"Okay, how about this?" Per asked, turning around to display his smooth ass and gorgeous back and legs. Now Sander had a new problem. He was completely and retractably as hard as a fucking rock.

"Great! Seriously, uh, really cute butt," Sander said, dry mouth completely overtaking him now. He felt strange, like he was on some kind of drug. Then Per turned back around and revealed the monstrous erection he had grown.

"Look! Now I'm at attention! My soldier's ready to fight, Sander!" Per chuckled. "What do you think of that?"

"Well, yeah. It's big. So, yeah, you're fine, Per. You won't have any trouble," Sander replied. "So is that all?"

"Yeah, man! Thanks! I'll go to where I'm sleeping and take care of this bad boy!"

"You do that!" Sander laughed. "See you in the morning."

"See you! And thanks, man! I appreciate it!"

"Goodnight, Per."

Per exited the room, gently and quietly closing the door behind him. Sander scooted himself back onto the thick, heavenly comfortable mattress. He punched and arranged the pillows to his liking, and then stretched and laid back, feeling the cool comfort of the eiderdown draped across his body.

Sander closed his eyes and drew in a deep, long, soothing breath. Then he grabbed his still-hard cock and pounded it into sexual bliss, the naked images of Per Larsen dancing through Sander's head. There, Per was being manipulated into every sexual position and homosexual act that the human male is able perform. And Johnnie Paul Allen was nowhere to be found.

Chapter 11

BASE CAMP TIVOLI

By THE TIME I WAS DONE SETTING UP MY

galley kitchen at the base camp, it had become a thing of beauty. I realize that beauty is in the eye of the beholder, of course, but anyone entering my storage tent would appreciate the organization and the relatively varied cooking ingredients I now had at my fingertips. These boys were going to eat well and heartily.

"Hey, Johnnie?" came a voice outside my tent flap.

"Come in," I said, pulling the flap away and recognizing the friendly face of Andy Kay, one of the Australians. "Can I get you anything? Some tea maybe?"

"Oh, yeah, that'd be ace, mate!"

"Pot's about to boil. Take a seat," I told him.

"What's on for brekkie?" Andy asked.

"Scrambled eggs, hashed potatoes, and sausages!" I replied with a smile.

"You're takin' the piss, yeah?"

"Nope. That's the menu," I assured him. "It'll be ready soon. In the meantime, your tea's up."

Andy sat with me while I kept the food going and spoke a little about what he thought might happen in the coming hours. It turned out the men hadn't been truly read in on the exact order of battle yet. They knew something major was afoot—the gear they'd brought told them that much. But now, having been in Ukraine since the day before, they each knew that it wouldn't be too much longer before the captain and the major would gather everyone together for The Briefing.

"You live in Denmark, do you?" Andy asked. While I put the egg mix together, and counted out the sausages, I filled him in on the life of Johnnie Allen such as it was. It was a fun way to incite some wonderful memories of the family, my wonderful man, and even little Jannik waiting for me back home.

"So is this Sander of yours a real looker?"

"Oh, God yes!" I told him.

"Where'd you meet her?"

"Well..." (Here we go.) "I met *him* at a party a few years back, and *he* turned out to be my complete and total soul mate. And I think he thinks I'm his. At least I hope so, anyway," I said.

"Ah! Good on you, mate. Most don't know how lucky they are to find 'The One', ya know? God knows I've not discovered mine. Don't know as I ever will, based on this job I have," Andy explained. Wow! Andy was totally cool. Being the manly Aussie bloke that he was, I'd have expected at least a half a rasher of shit from him. See...? Proves that stereotypes are usually wrong.

"What made you go into Special Forces?" I asked him.

"Honestly? It pays triple what I'd get in any other ANZAC force. I even looked at the navy, but nobody could beat the pay. I was top in gunnery and marksmanship, so here I am," he explained. "Plus, I get to off bad guys. So it has its attractions."

"Awesome. Hey, you wanna give me a hand?" I asked. He did, so I pulled together all of the hash packets and had him mix them with water in the big baggies. "Add just a bit of that non-dairy creamer and they'll be first cabin!"

"Crikey! I been on lotsa ops and I don't recall fine dining ever being a part of it, mate," Andy exclaimed. "This is awesome, as you Yanks like to say."

"Well, you know what they say about an army travelling on its stomach. You boys need your calories," I joked. "I'm gonna set that little folding table up like a buffet right here in front of the tent flap. It'll be ready in about fifteen minutes if you wanna go put the guys on notice," I told him. Andy practically skipped out of the tent, obviously looking forward to being the bearer of good news. And while I certainly wasn't overjoyed by the

171

reason we were there, I have to admit it felt like we were on a campout or scout trip. Dare I say I was loving it?

"RIGHT, FELLAS, LET'S GIVE OUR JOHNNIE a big hand for that lovely breakfast," Captain Lanning told the men. "It was better than my wife's cooking, I can assure you!" he smiled. The guys let off excited praise and I have to admit that I hadn't felt so proud in quite awhile. And the funny thing is, it was just so damned easy to pull off. And it made sense. Plus, I think it created a bit of an *esprit de corps.*

"So the time has arrived," Lanning continued. The men's bearing shifted completely. Instantly. It was about to become serious. "We are here to remove three very bad players from this world," Lanning began. "These men needlessly, and without compunction, terminated the lives of three hundred innocent civilians. They did this when they brought down Malaysian flight MH-17 last year."

The surprise reaction of the group quickly changed to resolution. Now they knew why there was a mixed force from multiple allies. This was a job that would be a pleasure to do.

"Our governments did their best to bring these men to justice, but the Russians would have none of it," Lanning continued. "The U.N. did their weakest best as usual, and you can imagine what that was like. So it falls upon us," Lanning explained. "And frankly, I'm honored to be a part of this."

That brought a positive response, and the briefing soon turned to Ops planning. Operation Dutch Oven was to commence that very night.

"DIDN'T SEE THAT COMING, did you, mate?" Andy asked me after. In fact, I had seen it. Funny how the driver-cook knew more about the mission than the men who would be executing it, but that's what need-to-know is all about. It was my job to get them safely in and out of the operations theatre, and in order to know the level of transportation protection they would need, I had to be read into it from the start. But I didn't let Andy know that. It would kind of piss me off if I was him, with the twenty-something American kid knowing more about Dutch Oven than he did.

"Yeah, wow, who'd have thought you guys would get to teach ol' Putin and his thugs a lesson like this?" I said. "It's so rare that you get to see the karma dessert get served up first hand."

"You've got that right, mate," Andy agreed.

"How've your MRX's been going today?" I asked him. An MRX is a Mission Rehearsal Exercise. They'd been practicing their breaches and kill tactics for most of the day, and Andy reported that it wasn't going to get any better. They were as ready as they were ever going to be.

"It's all good, mate. Them fuckers are enjoying their last day on earth," Andy reported. "I know the Dutch major will be getting with you after mess to coordinate our movements to the KZ's. There's three of them." KZ's are Kill Zones—the locations where the bad players are to be schooled.

Tonight's mission was going to be very exacting because there were three KZ's. Normally there would be three separate teams, with three separate transport vehicles, that would converge on the three targets simultaneously. Timepieces would be synchronized, and the teams would bust in and take out the targets all at once. This would ensure that there is little chance of any one target catching wind of the impending doom that was headed his way.

In this case, the kills would take place consecutively, which meant that technically the last guy to be visited could get wind that something bad was going down and scatter like a cockroach. Unlikely, but possible.

"Do you know when you go?" I asked.

"Zero-dark-thirty," he chuckled. "Around two or three, I'd expect. You'll know before we do. But Lanning told us to get some sleep in the meantime. So I'm off to dreamland, mate."

"Cheers!" I told him. "See you at showtime."

IT A BEEN QUITE THE COUPLE OF DAYS for Sander and Per. They were lodged in all things Parkour, and they had stayed so late on practice day that it was decided Per would stay over one more night.

After a rehash of the day, and some goof-off time with Jannik, the house settled into a quiet evening. Jannik headed off to bed, and the newfound friends did their best to recall some school events from back in the day that held at least some kind of commonality for them. Although admittedly there weren't many.

Per peppered Sander with a slew of questions about life as a gay man. It was funny, thought Sander, how the big cheese from school knew so little about one of the most important pieces of who he was. It's what being a gay Muslim must be like, he figured. They know they prefer men; the problem is that they don't know what to do about it.

Sander was experiencing a problem of his own. He found himself more and more attracted to the physicality of Per as each hour wore on. And the two were each on their third beer, so that didn't help matters very much.

"Sander! I have a job for you!" Per said with a chirp in his voice. "And you can't say no because there's no law against it!"

"What is it, *Per*-kour?!" Sander laughed.

"Perkour! Yes! That's my name now! I... Am... PERKOUR!" Per let out a buzzed laugh, and Sander chimed right in. A couple of pals; a couple three beers!

"What may I help the Great Perkour with?

"You see this?" Per said, grabbing a banana out of the fruit bowl on the side table. Per stood up and dropped his shorts, revealing once again his perfect, smooth ass. "I need butt fucking practice. I have never butt fucked! But if I am to be gay, dear friend, I must learn how to butt fuck! Soooo.... You will stick this in my butt just like it is my sexy lover's cock! And I will learn all I need to know about what it feels like to be butt fucked...by a banana!"

"You're crazy, man!" Sander laughed.

"No! No no no no!!! Sander, I am not crazy! I am bananas!"

"You fucking loser!" Sander joked. "This is what it means when somebody says Go fuck yourself!"

"Perhaps. But you have to come right here and stick this banana in my bottom! Right now, Sander Hansen! This is an order!" Per said, holding the banana out for Sander to (he hoped) take.

"Alright! But don't say I never did anything for you. And this banana will be on your cereal tomorrow!" Sander replied. "Bend over!"

Per grabbed his knees and bent over as far as he could, the position naturally spreading his butt cheeks as he did. Sander spit on the banana, and then spit on the ends of his left fingers. And he made physical contact with Per for the first time when he placed his spitty fingers on

Per's asshole, and butt crack. Sander had crossed the line at that moment.

Then he found himself getting hard as he took his hand and spread Per's crack open while he guided the banana into place. Surprisingly, Per took it well and within seconds Sander had planted the banana nearly three quarters of the way in.

Sander slowly began to move the banana in a steady, rhythmic motion and immediately Per popped a boner and began to moan. He was loving it.

The result of this was that Sander was turned on like a light switch. Per started stroking his own stiff cock while Sander increased the motion and the intensity of the ersatz dildo. The faster he went, the hornier Sander became.

Without a second's thought, Sander's pants wound up around his ankles, and he started jacking off. About every fifth stroke would find Sander's rock hard dick brushing past or along Per's right butt cheek. Now Sander was hot, and there would be no calm or cool until he'd released his warm load of semen. Now he thought of dumping it into Per's waiting ass crack. Of all things, for his own cum to land in the ass of the boy he'd coveted for so long.

"Oh, fuck! Sander! Keep going, man! This is fucking great!" Per whispered with passion. "Oh fuck! I can't believe I've missed this!"

"Feel good?" Sander breathed. "You like it?"

"Fucking great! Harder, man! Faster!"

Long Before Morning

Sander picked up the pace and Per moaned in kind. Sander couldn't believe his eyes, of course. A big, yellow banana was invading the man's ass, while he watched him crank his cock like nobody's business. He was so erect and so hard that it looked like he had been circumcised. Per's foreskin had completely retracted, and his head and surrounding areas were so clean that he truly appeared to be cut. And Sander wasn't the only one glancing at a hard dick and bouncing balls.

Since Sander had first dropped his shorts Per hadn't taken his eyes off of him. He was so turned on by seeing Sander jack off that it just added more passion to his own stiffie.

"You look fucking awesome, dude!" Per said, feeling his orgasm building to its crescendo. "That is one hot cock!"

"I'm gonna cum in your ass, Per. Is that okay?"

"Fuck yeah! *Fuck yeah!*" Per responded. He backed up closer to Sander and could feel his ass quivering in anticipation. Sander yanked the banana out and stood right behind Per, awaiting that most incredible of all physical feelings.

Per took it as a cue. He backed his ass down onto Sander's raging cock, and then reached around behind them both and grabbed each of Sander's butt cheeks. When he could feel Sander about to release, he pulled Sander's body as close (and as deep) as he could. Sander immediately came, his cum squirting square into Per's waiting ass. Per could hold it no more and came in four or five large squirts, squeezing the last drops onto his hand.

The two caught their breath, and after the drying and disposal of the cum towels was complete, the two sat down at the kitchen table. The young men wouldn't speak of their fun time together. What would be the point of that? But deep in the shadow of the service stairwell, adjacent to the kitchen, stood someone who might. That was because Jannik had witnessed everything since the insertion of the banana dildo. He had seen it all.

JANNIK HAS REALLY BEEN ACTING strangely today, and I just don't get it. Yesterday he was fine. Today he won't even talk to me. Maybe it's part of his whole Asperger's thing. Every time Johnnie goes away some dumb thing happens like this. I tried talking to Mama about it and she said what she always says: Give it time.

I thought he likes hanging around with me. Maybe we'll go see a film, or go to the beach, or just watch television. But today he acts like I smell bad.

"Spiderman! Come down here!" I call to him. He's been upstairs in his music studio all morning.

Didn't say two words at breakfast. "I want to talk to you!"

"Maybe I don't want to talk to you, asshole!"

"Hey! What the fuck! Get down here!"

"Go fuck yourself!" he yelled. What in the hell is going on? Jesus Christ in a Bath House, I can't believe this shit.

"Mama, sorry to bother you again about the beast, but he just called me an asshole and told me to go fuck myself!" I said into the phone.

"Gotta call your mommy, stupid child?" Jannik spewed as he walked right past me and headed for the door.

"Did you just hear him, Mama?!" Jannik was turning the door handle when he was stopped by the most effective brakes known to man: I held the phone toward him at arm's length, "Mama wants to talk to you. Now!"

"Fine!" he bellowed, as he stomped over and snatched the phone from my hand. "Hello, Mama, it's Jannik."

I know it is. I recognize the voice. What I don't recognize is the kid behind *the voice. What's the matter?*

"Can't say."

Did your brother say something to hurt your feelings? Why are you angry with him?

180

"No. And I can't say."

Can't or won't?

"Won't. He knows what he did. And until he tells me that he knows, I have not one thing to say to him," Jannik swore. "And I mean it, Mama."

I can hear that you do. Do you want to come here to the house?

"I can't. Sorry. Everything's fine," Jannik said.

I think you should come home. If you're just going to fight with Sander that can't be any fun for either of you.

"No, I want to stay until Johnnie comes marching home."

You miss Johnnie? Is that why you're upset, cowboy?

"Mama, can I go now?"

Only if you two promise to get along. Otherwise, I'm coming to get you. Understand?

"Okay. Here's Sander. I love you with kisses and candy." Jannik passed the phone to me, and again headed for the door. I told Mama I'd call her if he got out of hand or became even more disrespectful. And that was that.

Chapter 12

ZERO HOUR

So THIS IS WHAT WENT DOWN: TO SAY

that it was unlike anything I could have imagined would be the biggest understatement I could ever make. First off, it's nothing like in the movies. Well, most Special Ops movies, anyway.

Step one was for the team leader, the captain, and the major to perform and do a dry run of the route. I learned that we had operatives in place that were tracking every daily movement of the targets.

The intel was good. So we drove. The first location, code named Target Bethel Green, was located about ten kilometers outside of Kiev. The access road would likely be deserted when the visit was paid. The only contentious ingress would be the long, gravel drive to the house. Gravel makes a lot of noise. Especially in the dead of night.

"What ya think, lads?" Lanning asked no one in particular. The major wasn't keen, and neither was the Team Leader. "Be a right mess if they have a dog."

"Forget the dog," I ventured. "The gravel will do us in."

"What do you suggest then?"

"Let's leave ten minutes earlier and I'll drop you up the road. You can be all Special Ops sneaky and hoof it in. Then I'll come and get you when you're done," I said.

"Out of the mouths of babes, yeah?" Lanning teased the major. "I'll buy it." The major smiled and nodded his agreement. First job ready.

Next we drove in and across town to a second rural location—Target Paddington—but this one wasn't isolated. Adding to that, it wasn't a house. It was an auto repair shop, and to say it was the domain of even a shade tree mechanic would be a mighty exaggeration. It was a dump. Rusted out car bodies, antiquated equipment, and absolutely no doubt that a very unfriendly dog guarded it like the Taj Mahal.

"What about that ugly mutt?" I asked.

"Two ways we can handle it," Lanning replied. "We either silence it with a silencer, or we hit it with a dart. It'll depend on what we have back at Tivoli," he explained. "Right. What do you make of it?" Lanning asked the Team Leader.

"I think we draw him out. That's the safest way to protect the integrity of the job in my opinion," T.L. said. "Getting him outside should be easy enough."

I had a thought from the perspective of egress. I mean, we had to get everyone safely away from each job, making certain that we never compromise the next location. "Major? Captain? Can I give you something you might want to consider?"

Both quickly nodded and all eyes were on me. Dang. Better not sound like a clown right about now.

"The third location is in town," I began. "But this place is only seven clicks away from Tivoli. If we do this one, and then backtrack into town, that adds seven more clicks, and when we head back to base it'll be a total of twelve. Why don't we make this the last one, and from here head straight for home. Even if the cops get called, it'll take them some time to get out here. Not so much in town."

"What do you think, Captain?" the major asked

Lanning. "Why did the ground spooks suggest this order?"

"I can tell you why," I said. "It's one of those things that look great on paper, but when you're in the room you can see it's riskier than you first thought. Look here," I said, pulling out an actual, real, paper map. "If you use GPS, it'll tell you that the drive time at three k.p.h. over posted speeds will get us there faster. True that. But what our satellite friend doesn't know, and can't account for, are the number of traffic lights in the district that location number two sits in."

"Yeah? So how much time you reckon we can save?" T.L. asked.

"At least fifteen minutes total. At least. Every one of these intersections through here is an "A" road. Count 'em. There's one-two-three-four... There's nine of them. And every one of those intersections has left turn signals in all directions."

"Where does it indicate that on the map?" Lanning asked.

"It doesn't. I checked each intersection out when we were driving over here. And the ring roads, and the access roads on either side of us are one-ways. So, that's slow. No way to figure the time. We can figure

186

distance easy enough, but not how long it'll take," I explained.

"But don't we have to take that road anyway?" the major asked.

"Sure, but it'll only be one time. Next leg takes us from where we're at now, straight back to the barn. Where we wait. And eat tasty rations until it's safe to boogie out of Dodge," I said.

""What's boogie out of--"

"Sorry! It's a thing my granddad says. It means when we head back to Copenhagen. Anyway, that's just a thought, but I wanted to pass it by you," I concluded. It took three seconds.

"We take Johnnie's route," the Team Leader decided. "The quicker we can be done and out, the better I feel about it." And so that was that. Target Piccadilly would be the second stop.

Next step would be the real deal. Sweat. Shortness of breath. Heart pounding out of our chests. No margin for error. Life or death. And if all goes according to plan, three very merciful deaths for some very bad men. Our signal to Vladimir Putin that he'd better knock it off with the stupid dreams of a return to the Soviet empire. Not gonna happen, Vlad.

"GENTLEMEN. THIS IS IT. I HAVE NO doubt that we'll take care of business and return here together, job well done," Lanning said, rallying the troops. "Your training, and the fact that what we are doing is the right thing, will carry us through the next two hours and twenty minutes. Now, without threat of reprisal or separation from your home units, is anyone standing before me not in agreement with what we are about to execute? If you are, please step forward and you may remain behind," he explained.

Nobody so much as flinched. Lanning waited a full thirty seconds and the men seemed to become steelier. They were ready to exact the revenge response that the situation called for, and they were proud to do it.

"Like I even had to ask. Thank you, men. I also want to acknowledge a team member who has already shown us his value, but never more than earlier this evening when we settled on the mission route. Johnnie Allen is a professional through and through, and would that I could have him on every mission I'm ever a part of," Lanning said.

I thought he hated me when we first met at the embassy. And I had to do everything in my power to keep from crying like a little girl. I already felt so honored and proud of my profession. But this? I was completely taken aback. I experienced something that in my wildest dreams I could never expect. I was focused on Lanning when he said those wonderful words, but he met my eye and indicated with a slight nod that I should look off to my right. I did. Eleven members of one of the most elite groups of Special Ops in the whole world were standing at attention, saluting me. *Fuck!*

It all lasted mere seconds, and to them it was what it was. But to me? I now know there will be three things my mind will see as it shuts down the final time and I pass over to whatever's next. I will see Sander's face, his smile and his China blue eyes; I will see Benny and Maisey and Jannik, enthusiastic, playful, and kind; and I will see and feel this moment: The time that I was appreciated and saluted by a group of professionals that any of us would pray to be like. And now it was Zero Hour. We're away.

Chapter 13

WARPATH

JANNIK HANSEN WAS CRUSHED. SIMPLY gutted. He could never unsee it. Ever. For a few minutes, while it was happening, he wondered if in fact he'd lost his mind. That he was hallucinating somehow.

The worst part for Jannik was that he had to keep it all inside him. There was no one he could discuss it with, and he knew for damned sure that he wasn't going to destroy Johnnie by reporting what he'd seen. No, best to get it to stop. Best to make sure that it could never happen again. And it had to happen before Johnnie came home.

But where to take it? Should he confront his brother straight on? He was so flummoxed and near-desperate that he did the dumbest thing he could have done in the middle of such a crisis: of all things he took it to a Facebook friend, who immediately told another friend, which then circled back to him within hours. And the advice he thought he needed and received was as useless as, well, Facebook.

He decided he'd bide his time. He'd show no mercy, that was for sure. His brother was going to feel the wrath. He might be too stupid to know why, Jannik thought, but it was no longer going to be nice-kid-brother-business-as-usual for now. He'd figure it all out on his own eventually—exactly what he should do. But for now, Sander was going to experience the unforgiving specter of all out nuclear war. It was time for the official first strike.

He'd already sent a warhead across Sander's bow and it had freaked him out enough to cause him to phone their mother. Now it was time to send the *Enola Gay* over the idiot head of the Hansen gay and drop a few. Sander Lars Hansen, prepare to die a thousand deaths.

Per Larsen was gone, thank fuck, so it was down to him and Sander. He walked into the great room where his brother was intensely watching *The X-Factor* on television. He stood in front of the screen and blocked the view.

"What's your fucking problem, asshole?" Sander demanded. "Move your ass!"

Jannik stayed put.

"I mean it! Move!"

Jannik stood like a statue.

"Goddamn it, Jannik, move your fucking ass!" Sander yelled. "What's wrong with you?!"

"What's wrong with *you?!*" Jannik hissed.

"Move!"

"Make me!"

Sander rose to the challenge and was quickly on his feet. He just forgot about the coffee table when he made his play for Jannik and tripped straight onto it. It hurt his knee, and he stepped on the Blu-ray remote and broke it. And when he recovered from the fall enough to look Jannik in the eye with red rage, he was met with a hocking, three-ounce loogie right in the face. Jannik had spit on him like a Dilophosaurus delivering a load of venom. Then he ran like a rabbit.

Sander chased after him, but he was still caught off balance by the fall, and his angry brother was outside the house and long gone before he could recover.

"Mama, it's Sander," he barked into the phone.

"Hi, Pokey. What's wrong?" Mama replied.

193

"Come and get the little shit. He's crazy! Come and get him now!"

———————————————

THE EERIE QUIET; THAT'S WHAT surprised me the most. From the moment Lanning called the men into formation, not another word was spoken. He would point, and four guys would group together. Point again, four more. He did it a third time, and again another grouping of four appeared.

They were loaded for bear. The dark, matte-finish of the weapons slung over their shoulders reflected none of the ambient light. It was far from a full moon, and it was the blackest part of the night. The air was warm, and the motorway could be heard very far off in the distance, and only because the sound carried farther and clearer by night.

To look at the men, one would never guess they were about to embark on a government sanctioned killing mission. They were ready for work, not unlike any of us who head for our jobs each day. This was their job, and by all indications they were good at it.

Lanning gave me a nod, and mimed turning the ignition. I opened the side doors of the van, and then walked around to the driver's side and took my place. The van started right up, and moments later I could feel the movement created by the men taking their seats. Again, it was the quiet that I found so fascinating. Their weapons didn't offer up any sound; no clanking, or stray thuds of rifle butts, or any sound at all.

Even the ruffling of their black tactical clothing was muted, probably from the armor vests; still, it all took on a kind of dreamlike quality because when you're used to how something is supposed to be, even concerning sounds, such changes play tricks with your mind. I think they rely on that fact to get the upper hand on their targets.

"Clock has started," Lanning announced. "Team leader, you have the team."

The T.L. responded with two squelches on his radio. None of the men would utter a word until the mission was completed, and we were on our way back to base. I just drove. My adrenal glands were certainly functioning to capacity, I might add. It was exhilarating, and my vision was hyper clear. My breath felt cool, and though my heart rate was elevated, I felt top of the world. I wasn't breathing any harder, and I felt unusually calm. Even a touch giddy.

The drive to the first target took exactly twenty-seven minutes, forty-three seconds. A little under three minutes early. Good. We could bank that time if needed.

I stopped the van at the pre-designated spot, and Action Team One left the van and walked aggressively toward their destination. We could see the house plain as could be. There was no cover. No tree screening. No outbuilding to shield the men from anyone who would care to glance in our direction from one of the windows. Yet all that, and we could barely see them.

They hunched down in such a way, and moved so completely as a unit, that they actually appeared to be nothing more than a shadow. Granted, they were on the move. But had a light appeared in the house, or they felt someone may be watching them, were they to freeze in place you'd never see them. They'd disappear.

While this was happening, the men of Action Group Two left the confines of the van and stood just off the back right of the vehicle. This was in anticipation of Group One's return. The Group One guys would take the seats of the Group Two's once they returned. Then the Two's would take the seats by the doors, ready for their stop. It would repeat itself for the Group Three team. Clockwork. Precision.

"Dog One is put down. Repeat, Dog One has been eliminated," came the quick and terse radio communication.

"One down, two to go," Lanning said to us. Less than three minutes later we were away from the first target location and headed for the next.

This location was at an apartment block in the middle of Kiev. The target was some guy called Claude, or something like that. He was the one who had actually launched the missile at the plane, according to the intelligence briefing that the first guy—the colonel that the team had just taken down—had filed with the Kremlin.

The apartment was situated over an alley archway that led into an area behind the building. The major indicated that I should back all the way under the arch and park in the shadow that it cast. Smart! Because the streetlight hanging over the center of the narrow road was the source of the shadow, so the shadow would never change. We were effectively parked in the dark.

Action Group Two scurried quietly from the van and breached the common door in the back garden. Quiet as mice in a cheese factory, the men ascended the stairs and were soon out of sight. One minute. Two minutes. Five minutes. Seven. Had something gone wrong?

The second the thought crossed my mind the back cargo doors of the van opened up and we felt a heavy 'thunk' on the van floor. The doors were quickly shut, and the team hopped into the van. We were away. Not a single car or pedestrian was seen.

"Dog Two down?" Captain Lanning asked. His answer arrived in the form of a very enthusiastic thumbs up from my mate, Andy. "Do we have a guest?" Lanning asked. Two of the team nodded. That's what the thunk must have been.

I drove to the ring road and took it in the opposite direction from the second target area. That's because even though technically it was a further two kilometers, all of the lights were set to green this time of night. Therefore the running time was quicker, and there was much less chance of running into a cop, too.

Our guest on the back floor was none too happy, but no one seemed to care, so I didn't either. I would later learn that she was the target's girlfriend and had been staying the night at his apartment. When the team realized this, they shot a short term tranquilizer into her neck and then waited a few minutes for her to become inert. That's what had cost the extra time.

After they eliminated the bad guy, they shoved her into a body bag and carried her to the van. She had now just woken up and was admittedly complaining just a tad. She had no idea how lucky she was.

Once they'd dealt with number three we would deposit her in some isolated rural location before heading back to Tivoli. She was already blindfolded and bound at the hands, so she wouldn't see us as we drove away. And chances were very favorable that she would get herself to safety soon enough.

"DO YOU WANT TO TELL ME exactly what is going on between you and your brother?" Mama asked Jannik as they drove to the family house. "This isn't like either of you."

"Nothing to tell, really. Your son is an asshole," Jannik replied without emotion.

"Which one?" Mama chuckled.

"The other one."

"Well, you'll have to do better than that," Mama

199

said. "I've known you both for your whole lives and I have never seen anything like this. The things you said to him were just awful, Jan. There's no excuse for that, is there?" Mama said. "I mean, really..."

They joined the motorway and were soon up to speed. This time of night was dominated by semis loaded with farm goods, machinery, and cargo containers from Esbjerg and as far away as Aarhus. The occasional German license plate could be spotted as well.

"If you won't tell me what happened, how can I help you?" Mama added. "You know, this is very frustrating for a parent. And don't forget, I'm the parent."

"What about Pop?" Jannik asked.

"Well, he kind of is. Though sometimes I wonder if he's not just another one of my kids. That man is wonderful, but sometimes..."

"...You just want to spank him?" Jannik grinned.

"Like you need right now!" Mama smiled.

"I don't need the spanking, Mama. The other boy does."

"So you keep telling me, but you won't say why!"

"That's because it's up to him to say. So ask *him*, why don't you?" Jannik concluded. Mama released a frustrated *eeeggghhh!* and finally admitted to herself that she was talking to The Great Wall of Jannik. She knew that whenever the wall went up, the communication went down, so she decided to table the discussion for another time. And hopefully this would all resolve itself soon and the boys could go back to being the best friends they'd always been.

"NEGATIVE CONTACT!" the Team Leader reported. The first thought—the first fear, actually—was that somehow Target Paddington had been tipped off. Very reliable intel that was barely three hours old put the target snug as a roach right here. He should be *here.*

"Come on back. We'll reassess," Captain Lanning replied over the secure comm link. In seconds the men were back in the van. A quick options evaluation ensued.

"What's our safe time?" T.L. asked.

"Twenty-four minutes."

"You think he's hiding?" the major asked.

"Negative. The scene was blue and sterile," T.L. replied. That means that the place didn't look as though the occupant had done a scramble or a quick dash. There was no warm, half drunk coffee cups; no smell of cigarettes; inappropriate lights left burning; no television on. No smell of body odor or even indications of body heat. The guys know what to look for to indicate a runner, and there was none here. He was just gone.

"So we'll wait for him, and if he doesn't show before the clock runs out we'll just have to take our chances later, or maybe today's his lucky day," Captain Lanning decided. So we waited.

I clicked on my red light night vision pen—when activated it gives out red light like the kind you see in submarine movies—and examined my trusty map. I noticed something on it and without a word I leaned over to Captain Lanning and pointed at what I saw.

He took the map in hand and pored over it, then let out kind of an *I can't believe this* chuckle. He glanced in my direction and gave me a quick nod and a smile.

"Boys, we're gonna take a little side trip," Lanning announced. I fired up the van and aimed it at the road. In about one and a half clicks there it stood. The local bar pub, lit up and noisy, just as a watering hole anywhere on the globe should be. The hope was that our prey would at this moment be inside imbibing his last drink.

"Okay, Johnnie, go get a beer," Lanning said. He handed me his phone. A picture was already displayed on it. "There's your man. See if he's in there pissing away Putin's money. We'll wait right here for you, lad."

I went into the pub where the plan was to head for the toilet so I could get my bearings. But I didn't have to.

Just as I opened the door I saw that I was face-to-face with Eugeny Kuzmich. He brushed right past me as he left the pub.

I had to continue into the pub or it would appear unnatural, so I did go for the toilet as planned. I waited about a piss-length, and returned to the van.

"He's here," I said. "Actually, he's headed down the road for home."

"You sure?" T.L. asked me.

"Positive. He's wearing a dark green hoodie and I promise we'll drive right past him if we head for Paddington right now."

"What's your plan?" Lanning asked T.L.

"Let's go get him."

I pulled onto the road and headed for the location; sure as shit, there he was. He wasn't exactly staggering, but you could tell he'd downed a few.

We passed him at regular driving speed, and as

203

soon as we'd rounded the final curve before the original target location, T.L. asked me to turn the van around and stop.

"Let me out here. Keep the motor running, and turn the headlights to bright." T.L. said. He left the van and stood in the road in front of the van. T.L. sauntered right up to him.

"Eugeny! Put your hands in the air!" T.L. demanded in perfect Russian. Eugeny stopped in his tracks and threw his hands up.

"What the fuck do you want?!" The T.L. shot him point blank with a silenced handgun, pumped a few *just in case* bullets into him once he hit the ground, and calmly rejoined us. But not before he'd snapped a pic of the now expired Eugeny looking very much like road kill.

When we got about half a kilometer from the main road junction, he had me pull over again, this time to set the girl out. Once we had finished that last bit of business, we were on the "A" road back to Tivoli.

Three very bad players had been retired from the chess board. Operation Dutch Oven was over — a success — and soon it would be time to get back home to little Denmark.

Chapter 14

JOURNEY HOME

THERE ARE CERTAIN TRICKS THAT ARE

employed in order to ensure that no adversary has the opportunity to adjust to your way of doing business. In the case of egress in an exfiltration, this is particularly important. Think about it. You've just walked into his domain and did whatever you came to do. He's not happy at all. This will also be the time when all the stops are pulled and the police and the military—especially at border crossings—go nuts.

An emotional response like that is actually preferred because when they're angry, they get stupid.

That said, I have to consider that the lower the man on the totem pole, the less likely they'll make a mistake. That's because they're usually not as emotionally invested as their superiors are. So while Putin and his henchmen are throwing teacups and calling their mommies up at the Kremlin, back here in real world the workaday customs official or street cop can actually spot things with heightened clarity.

Now try explaining that to the crew that you're babysitting. See, for them the job's over. I'll bet if I passed out airline tickets afterwards and told them to phone a cab to the airport they wouldn't think twice about showing up at the Aeroflot check-in counter for the noon flight home. All well and good until the guys with the German Shepherds invite you for a little tête-à-tête in the back room behind the baggage claim.

No. That won't do at all. The boys did their jobs well, so now it was time for them to stand down and leave the driving to me, as the old saying goes.

"When do we bug out of Tivoli?" Major Vanderman asked me.

"Tomorrow for the border crossings, and then we start the trip back to Copenhagen," I told him.

"What do you mean by *start* the trip? Seems kind

of nebulous," Vanderman said. "Aren't we just going to drive back?"

"Not exactly. Should we get the T.L. and Captain Lanning in on this so you'll all get an idea of what the plan is?"

"Yes. Let's do that."

Following the group debrief, the three officers joined me in my tent. Thankfully I'd taken the time to write up the plan so they would have it to review once our meeting was concluded. I also hoped they would agree to it. It is a military structure, and I was under the command of the major and the captain. If they wanted to haul out their thumbs and hitchhike home with a side trip to a German beer garden there was nothing I could do to stop them.

And coming off of the high of a successful mission can distort the fact that it's not really over until you're safely home. Many operatives have shelved the fact and have gone on to pay the price.

"Welcome, gentlemen. I'd like to brief you on what I believe is the best, safest way to get everybody home in one piece," I began. "It's multimodal, but it's safe. That's my primary concern, and I promise it'll work as proposed."

"Right, mate. Don't keep us in suspense," Lanning said. "We're all ears."

"You can bet that by morning they'll be in high gear over this. I don't think it'll be enough to close the border, especially that early in the game, but assuming that they'll up their presence on the Ukrainian side, we need to get out as unnoticed as possible," I began.

"Aren't we just going to drive out like we came in?" T.L. asked.

"No. We can't do that. They'll tear apart any vehicle that's not Uke. Even Russian and Polish plates are gonna be given the eagle eye. So forget the Dutch and Brit oil workers ruse. That's gone," I explained.

"So then tell us," Lanning said.

"This should be good," Vanderman added.

The plan as I saw it would mean putting relational distance between each member of the team. The opposition would be looking for anything out of the ordinary. And a clump of foreigners crossing into Poland would be a flag as red as the old commie banners that once flew on every street corner in Kiev. So it had to appear as if they didn't know each other.

"We're breaking the men up into single and up to three in a group. They'll cross at different times throughout the day and make their way to an address I'll give you. There we'll wait until the next part of the plan takes effect," I told them.

"Next, you'll take a combination of buses, a hired van, and even a couple of taxis to three different locations out of town. You'll stay there until I make contact with you and pick you up."

"Wait. Where will you be?" Lanning asked.

"Actually, if all goes well for me I'll be waiting for you there. Or I'll be there shortly," I said. "Once you're all safely out of Ukraine, I'll make my way to the central station in Kiev and ride the train to Warsaw. That's where I'll get the nice, big, comfy Loadstar van with the DVD player and everything and come collect your butts. Then we're away home."

"Sounds complicated," Vanderman declared. "But..."

"I'm with you, Major. If Johnnie thinks it best, it's what we'll do," Lanning said. "When do we inform the men?"

"Uhmm... How about after breakfast? Then we'll tear down and get going," I said.

"What about the gear?" T.L. asked.

"That'll stay in the van. A local who's with the Ukrainian Defense Force will come and take it all away once I call him from the station. It'll be safe until the Dutch embassy can put it all in a diplomatic pouch and get it out. Only thing you'll be taking is some beat up suitcases and gym bags with some clothes and stuff," I explained. "That's pretty much it. It really goes easier than it sounds."

"When does your train leave, then?" T.L. wondered.

"Quarter to ten tomorrow night. I'll pick up the van in Warsaw and then come back to gather up my little birds!"

With nods all around, they said goodnight. We would try and get in as much shuteye as we could before the journey home commenced.

JANNIK HAD FOLLOWED THROUGH on his threat to make Sander's life a living hell. He achieved it with the silent treatment.

His brother came to visit at the family home and his goal was to see if Mama had figured anything out. She hadn't. "Your guess is as good as mine. He's definitely upset, but he won't let any of us know why he is," Mama explained. "Are you sure you don't remember doing anything to make him mad?"

"I swear, Mama. I don't have a single clue. One minute everything's great. Per was over, and we had fun in town. Per thinks he's great. Then all of a sudden he's a total jerk to me," Sander explained.

"Do you think maybe he's upset because Per stayed the night? Maybe he thinks you're replacing Johnnie with Per?"

"Oh, Mama, that's stupid! He knows that's crap. Give him credit!" Sander exclaimed. "I mean, there's no reason... He, uh... *Shit!*" and Sander bounded up the stairs and burst into Jannik's room.

"You can knock, asshole!" Jannik spat when he saw his brother standing there. "Who said you could come in?!"

"Cowboy, I need to ask you something really important," Sander began. This got Jannik's attention. The young teen slowly rose from his bed where he had been reading *Anders And* comic books, and sat up, his piercing blue eyes shooting daggers at his brother.

"Go on..." Jannik prompted. "This should be good." Dr. Evil had nothing on Jannik Mads Hansen.

"You saw us, didn't you?"

Jannik held his gaze with Sander and then slowly began to nod, never changing his expression. Sander felt the wind completely knocked out of him

211

and next found himself sitting on the edge of Jannik's bed. "Why didn't you say anything?" Sander asked.

"I couldn't make myself talk. Don't be an idiot, Sander. Just don't," Jannik said in a voice so soft that it belied the usually exuberant lad whose heart was now broken. "What is the matter with you?"

"Promise you won't say anything. Can you do that?" Sander begged. Jannik was silent. "Cowboy?"

"Don't fucking cowboy me, you selfish fuck. If I don't say anything it'll only be because I don't want Johnnie hurt," Jannik said. "Not because I wanna help you out."

"I know. I get it. Sooo..."

"So fuck you. You know I'm not gonna tell him. But I swear, if you ever... I mean ever...--"

"--I won't! I promise, Jan! Please believe me, okay?"

Jannik quietly nodded and Sander sighed deeply. He was relieved, and he knew he could trust Jannik to keep his mouth shut for the very reason that Jannik had said—he didn't want to do anything that would hurt Johnnie. And Jannik knew that such a revelation would kill him, so for now Sander was safe.

"I'm not fucking around!"

"I know you're not. I do. So, thanks brother," Sander said.

"Don't *'brother'* me. Just leave, asshole," Jannik said before going back to his comic books. "Go tell Mama we kissed and made up. I don't need her to be all worried and stuff because of your bullshit."

"I will," Sander promised. When he reached the door he paused for a moment and turned to his brother. "So have *we*?" Sander asked.

"Have we what?"

"Have *we* kissed and made up?" The room was still. Sander couldn't see the expression on Jannik's face as it was guarded by the comic book.

"I'll think about it," Jannik replied. Then the boy gave him a quick wave out of the room. It would have been funny—Jannik shooting him one of those *"You may take your leave, slave,"* motions with his hand—were it not for the serious nature of the situation.

But Sander saw it as the first trace of levity since Jannik's freeze-out from yesterday. Once again, relief came to Sander. He'd dodged a very high caliber bullet, and he knew it.

Chapter 15

THE CROSSING

TIVOLI WAS CLEARED BY 1000 HOURS
and the team had staggered their arrival times at the border approximately ten to twenty minute intervals throughout the day.

The officers waited inside a border pub acting the part of useless, drunken layabouts. They ordered beer after lager after Ukrainian ale, with bad, greasy pub food to go with all of the alcohol. In reality they drank very little, instead pouring the amber liquids into a crack between the worn out banquettes and the wall.

The men would each make an appearance to let the officers know they were about to cross, and about

1930 hours they were getting down to the last couple of soldiers. That was Lanning's and Vanderman's cue to prepare for their own walk across the frontier.

Once each man had crossed the Ukrainian checkpoint and had entered no man's land—the few kilometers between there and the entrance to Poland—they would hail a taxi and get to the Polish side as quickly as they could.

In the meantime, I had taken a city bus into town and spent the day checking out the tourist trappings of central Kiev. I would have gone to a movie. Closed until evening. I would have gone to a mall; maybe I would have found a book store to burn up some daylight. Nope.

Ah! There had to be a museum, right? Sure! Open Wednesdays from 3 o'clock to seven; Saturdays from noon to five; alternate Sundays from noon to four.

Have I ever mentioned how much I despise the Cyrillic alphabet? Asian lettering made more sense to me.

I did ride the trolley line pretty much everywhere it went, and I had a pretty good lunch of Russian peasant food. It's really very tasty, and it was cheap. Pirozhki, which are these little bread buns stuffed with all kinds of things—meat, onions, carrots, mashed potatoes, mushrooms. Good stuff.

And I found a cart selling blini and syrniki, thin Russian pancakes with raisins, butter, fruit and topped with a dab of very cold sour cream. Why are the countries that are the most messed up always tend to have the best eats? India. Mexico. The entire Middle East?

Man, did the clock go slow that day. I mean each minute passed like five. But eventually the time arrived for me to head for the border pub and make sure that everyone was gone. I would stay there until eight o'clock and then get over to the central railway station.

I had to assume that all was well. None of the team were anywhere to be seen, so now I just had to get myself to Warsaw. Easy!

N O T I C E:
THE NIGHT TRAIN TO BERLIN
(VIA WARSAW)
HAS BEEN CANCELLED.

Oh, for shit's sake! Well, isn't that just how it goes?! No trains until morning. (**Maybe!**) So what's a poor lad to do? Okay, Allen, *think!* Bus? No. Nothing scheduled is moving. Airport? Maybe. But nothing until morning, though I wouldn't arrive by much later than I would have by train. That's one for the plus column.

There's one thing I can try first. Low risk. All they can really do is say no.

VYBACHTE. A KHTO Z VAS HOVORYAT' PO-anhliys'ky? "Excuse me... Do any of you speak English?" I mangled it, but I made sure to play the part of lost American college student as a sympathy ploy, and I hoped for the best.

I had crossed the entire station platform and found the workers' break room hoping I could hitch a ride on something—a mail train, milk train, even a freight train would do provided it was Warsaw bound. I was also relying on underpaid trainmen taking a stack of rolled western currency as an incentive.

The men stared solemnly and blankly at me, but a teenage kid in a boiler suit nodded my way and said he spoke a little English.

"My name is Johnnie. I'm trying to get to Warsaw...uh, *Varshava*..."

"Yes. Warsaw—yes. No more train now. Is kaput," he told me.

"Is there another train? Post train? Slow train?" I asked him. He quickly conferred with the old fellas and they responded with shaking heads that promised that the answer was no.

"You can go in morning, yes?" he asked me. I looked dejected and took a seat at the table.

"I must get to Varshava. May I pay money to ride a different kind of train?" I produced my wad of cash, hoping that good ol' capitalistic need would trump the rules a bit. The boy—I later learned his name was Ramey—indicated I follow him. Well this was it. Either my conveyance awaited, or I'd die with a bashed-in skull deep within the locomotive maintenance pits of the Kiev railway station.

But Ramey led me to another office and I could tell he had now become my advocate. The man in the office knew him well, and the ease of their conversation led me to believe that we may have something here.

"You. Boy. You coming from USA, yes?" the man asked.

"Yes, sir," I replied. "They cancelled the train and

I have to be in Warsaw in the morning to meet the rest of my classmates."

"Yes, but there is no train. If there is no train, there is no Warsaw for you, yes?" he explained.

"I see."

"Wait! Perhaps there is way for to get you to the Warsawa, and you go this tonight," he said. Ramey smiled. "But maybe costs this little bit of money, and I cannot say what happen in Poland. Maybe they not so understand like Tito and Ramey."

The plan was to ride in the guard's van of a mail train that was leaving within the hour. The Ukrainian crew would only ride to the border, however. Once in Poland, there would be a crew change and it would be up to the Polish trainmen whether I could remain aboard and ride it into Warsaw, or find myself left on the platform. I was game.

So after a few bills were passed over to Tito and Ramey, and another little stack placed in the care of the train conductor of *Mail and Package Express Nr. 19-07*, I found a seat in the railcar and hoped for the best. It was progress, anyway.

SUCCESS! TURNS OUT THE POLISH rail workers were very happy to have me along for the ride, and never even hinted at wanting graft. So I was in, baby! I would be in Warsaw by 10 o'clock in the morning, pick up the comfortable minibus, and beat cheeks back to Scuzzytown (that wicked excuse for the Polish side of the Ukrainian border) and scoop up my boys!

All went as planned. The credit cards worked. The fuel tank was full. And I was soon on the road again.

I tried giving Pokey a call, but he wasn't around so I thought maybe I could surprise him. I'd be home day after tomorrow—a full three days ahead of schedule—so why not have a little fun?

The drive was uneventful, and it felt so awesome to pull up to the safe house exactly as expected. I saw Lanning sitting in the garden, and the boys were barbecuing and kicking a football around. Many of them were just lying on the grass soaking up the summer rays listening to music.

About an hour after I arrived I got word that the UDF had grabbed the van and the gear and were safely in possession of the whole lot. The last vestige of Tivoli Base was wiped away. No one would ever know where the mission was launched from.

Long Before Morning

Moscow Center would be crying in their vodka for months after, especially when they'd receive the overnights that the ones responsible for this perfectly executed mission escaped detection and capture. In your sour, frowny face, Putin!

Our return route brought us to Berlin, where the Dutch and Australian parts of the team would go on their way. The Aussies would be flying home; the Dutch would ride the luxurious *City Night Line Express* train to Amsterdam.

The last five, my new British friends, would be dropped at their embassy in Copenhagen.

It was bittersweet bidding good-bye to the others, and there was the usual sniping and jocular joking amongst the team. But anyone could see that it was very much like the last day of summer camp when all of the new friends you've made must return to their regular lives. The mission was over.

Captain Lanning opened up as we drove the final leg from Berlin to Copenhagen. The men slept as we jetted down the autobahn towards home. One thing Special Ops guys know is that you never pass up a chance to sleep, eat, or shit when you're on an active mission. So that left Lanning and me.

"You know mate, I didn't mean anything by my reaction when you told me you had a fella; you know that you're gay," he said.

"I know. Besides, I can't have been the first one that you ever met before, right?" I chuckled. "We're everywhere these days, you know."

"I know," he laughed. "I am in the military, after all. I guess you just didn't act like... I mean, well, you know, all swishy and that," he explained. "You're just a regular bloke, yeah?"

"I think you'll find that more of us are than aren't."

"Yeah?"

"Absolutely," I told him. "When I met Sander that first night, I fell for him instantly. But I thought he was straight, so I didn't try anything, you know?"

"No kidding?"

"True. Funny thing was that he felt the same way about me, and he thought I was straight. So for a little over a year we were the best of friends, but neither knew that the other one was gay as can be. We were in complete and total love, but didn't move on it," I explained.

"How'd you finally break the stalemate?" Lanning asked.

"Sander did it. One night he just thought fuck it and took his chances. He told *me*, and you should've seen his face after I told him that I felt the same way,"

I said.

"Awww... Lovely story, that. Wish I had a similar one to tell you, but me and Mrs. Lanning had been together since we were fourteen. Same school, same church, same workingmen's club. We were eighteen and one day we were down the pub and she told me her sister was getting hitched to a mate of mine," Lanning told me.

"Oh, yeah?"

"Yeah. So she said we should probably go ahead and get married. We could have a double wedding and split the costs of the reception with her sister and my mate. So we did. Seven months later our daughter was born prematurely, if you get my drift. There were a lot of preemies born round my neighborhood in those years. Don't reckon it's changed much," Lanning explained. "I like your story much better."

"Yeah. And no premature births with us!" I reminded him.

"I should hope not!" he laughed.

"Guess that would make it a shitty proposition, yeah?" I joked. And we laughed our way down the autobahn, and to home.

Chapter 16

"JUST A QUICK DETOUR, CAPTAIN. I

promised my friend a little souvenir," I said, as we entered central Copenhagen. I turned onto the south ring road that took us toward Amager, and then the final jog into Freetown Christiania.

So here's a one hundred percent Danish tidbit that no one ever believes. Back home when I tell about it they accuse me of totally making it up. When I told my little brother about Christiania, he said that's where he wants to live when he comes over here for college.

Back in 1971 a bunch of hippies took over an old, abandoned military base and started a commune. They formed a government—they called it the Anarchist Community Government—and told the king and the government where they could stick it.

And they've been there ever since, living happy as hippies tend to do. And how did the Danish authorities handle it? They said, "Okay."

The place soon became a kind of tourist Mecca because hippies make cool art, music, and very tasty brownies! They had shows and cabarets, drag shows, and were very inclusive. People from all over the world came to see Christiania and many ended up just staying.

A very popular Danish pop star, Lukas Graham, was born and raised in Christiania and seems all the better for it. And in Christiania they started Bøssehuset—The Gay House—for gay activism, fun and over-the-top variety shows, parties, and legit theater.

But the thing that the little island country-within-a-country is most famous for? The Pot! They have the best weed anywhere, hands down. You think the Danes make great beer? You ought to toke up some Christianian cannabis! Christiania: The kind of Christian I like!

Well, after all, I did promise my buddy Tyrone the very best for all the contributions he made above and beyond the call of duty for Dutch Oven. So I was planning to be true to my word.

"I've heard about this place," Lanning said. "It's true they have hash tables and greenhouses and the like?"

"Yep! And I plan to pick up a few plants worth for me and my mate at the embassy," I admitted.

"Won't your bosses get their knickers in a knot over that?" T.L. asked from the back seat.

"I won't tell if you won't!"

I parked the van and crossed the entrance bridge into the village, and was back within minutes. Job well done.

"That was quick," Lanning observed. "I can't get in and out of Tesco's that fast!" He said with a grin.

"I got some brownies, too. Don't suppose anyone would care for one," I offered.

"Go on, then..." Lanning said. "Lads?" he said, eyeing them in the sunshade mirror.

"Smoke 'em while ya got 'em, ain't that what they say in the war movies?" T.L. joked. So I just tossed the bag behind me and let survival of the fittest determine who would be imbibing in brownies.

Half an hour later we were parked in front of the staff entrance gate for Her Majesty's Embassy in Copenhagen. And moments later I was saying good-bye to my 'new friends for life'.

Long Before Morning

I drove the few hundred feet back to our embassy and checked in, then headed over to the Central Railway Station and returned the van to Hertz. Half an hour later I was on the train home. I was officially clocked out. Operation Dutch Oven was no longer active and was headed for the archives.

JANNIK HAD BEEN AT HIS house for two days, and was planning to go back to the boys' place on Friday afternoon. Surely Johnnie would be home by then, he reckoned.

In the meantime he would continue reading his current book, *The Giver*, about a futuristic world where emotion was shuttered and perfection was anything but perfect. Its themes had grabbed him, and he couldn't put the Lois Lowry novel down for even a minute. He'd even fallen asleep with it in his hands the night before.

He was also enjoying spending some quality time with his cats, and scarfing down Mama's wonderful cooking. He ate well at the boys', that's for sure. But sometimes a homemade plate of Danish biksemad, or frikadeller and potato salad were the only dishes that could satisfy. And Mama always delivered. His Pop's waistline was proof of that.

He was also relieved about his handling of his brother's indiscretion with that guy from the parkour team. *Fuck that jerk! What the hell was he doing, getting into the middle of somebody else's marriage?* Jannik steamed. Of course, he also realized that it took two to tango. But still, if that fucker hadn't swung his dick in Sander's face things might have gone differently.

Jannik wondered what Johnnie's trip was about this time. He would tell as much as he could when he got home, but he knew that even if it was really dangerous, that Johnnie would never let on about it.

How was it? Jannik would ask.

Fine! would come the instant reply, nearly always accompanied by a big grin. Johnnie's smile was so reassuring, and that was the problem! Jannik could never tell if Johnnie was just masking some awful thing that might have happened just to protect him from the reality of whatever it was.

He had seen firsthand how his brother-in-law operates on the job. That happened a little over a year ago when Jannik had been kidnapped in a grudge payback by a crazy Russian. Mad at Johnnie for messing up his plans, the dude had instructed a very amateurish middle eastern terror cell to snatch the boy in exchange for (what turned out to be) very little aid from the Russians. The whole thing was stupid, but it wasn't at the time. Jannik thought he was a goner.

Then in walked Johnnie and a very nice lady from Iceland who stopped the bad guys and brought him home to the family on a really cool helicopter.

So anyone messing with Johnnie would forever find themselves on the receiving end of Jannik the Hell Child, as Sander Lars Hansen soon discovered. When it came to Johnnie, blood was never thicker than water, Jannik vowed.

Now it was time for sleep.

Jannik arranged the cats around his bed. Each had a special spot to sleep in, and they would usually make it all night without moving.

Lille Lort always took half the pillow, which Jannik really liked because she would keep his face warm, and she always purred for long periods. It was like having a fuzzy face massager.

Caspar would lay atop the eiderdown between Jannik' legs, just below his junk. Jannik called him the ball warmer.

And Farley always parked his fat tabby self against the instep of his human's right foot. And thus Jannik and his Three Amigos would pass the night into the next morning, ready to hit the deck running, or at least at a very steady walk! What a lucky kid indeed.

ALMOST THERE, ALMOST THERE, Johnnie Allen's almost there! One more step, one more foot, one more meter, and I'm here! YAY! I'm home! Dang, that last walk up the drive is murder!

So I know Jannik wants to see *San Andreas* this weekend because he thinks Dwayne "The Rock" Johnson is cool, which of course he is.

Pokey's gonna want to eat like a little piggy, so I guess I'll just have to help the bugger out and spoil him with some cool restauranting. Maybe the Italian place over on Jernbanegade. He can pick.

I'm in the house.

No one's home.

Upstairs to Jannik's studio loft.

Set his speakers on his mixing desk.

I'm tired from the walk.

231

Long Before Morning

Jannik's day bed sure looks inviting.

I accept the invitation.

I fall fast asleep; it feels wonderful.

Laughter. I hear laughter.

I sneak downstairs.

I round the corner.

I see them. I see them.

There is a guy who's going down on Pokey.

I die at that moment.

My heart. My soul. My life. It is extinguished.

I leave. I walk past them as I go to the front door.

They see me.

They scramble.

Sander Lars Hansen reaches out for me. He yells.

Stop!

Don't go!

This is what he says.

I keep going. The car is running and I go.

My life is over.

Why?

I was good to him.

I love him.

I am fair.

I am honest.

I live for him.

Why?

Chapter 17

THE FIRST WEEK

MY BRAIN IS SCRAMBLED. IT'S PURE
mush. I can't think straight. I can't feel; I feel too
much.

I had to leave town. Everywhere I look is
another memory, a reminder, a good time, love
realized and lost. I can't take it.

I cry. I'm worn out from crying. This can't
happen because it's just not right. Why would he do
this?

I can't trust him anymore. Ever. This isn't
betrayal; this is murder. Murder of the soul.

I have to call Grampy. He has to tell me that everything will be fine. Marge. I have to call work and tell them I'm done. No more. I have to quit the job, quit the country, and just go away.

There's Bertha Moon's house. I could go there. And, what? Tell her that another Hansen is worse than the piece of shit she's married to?

Jannik! What about him? Fuck this! This is just not fair!

Doesn't he see how much there is to lose here?

―――――――――――――――

I'M AT MARGE'S APARTMENT now, and I can't stop crying. I feel so bad for Marge having to hear this shit. She's just as shocked as me, and like me keeps searching for a reason to explain that I didn't see what I saw. But I saw it.

I stayed up most of the night and wrote a letter to the man I had pledged my heart and my life to. It was a senseless exercise, I was sure. But as a declaration, and for posterity's sake it mattered to me that I do it.

In a thousand, thousand years I would never have thought that such a letter would be crafted with my hand. But here we were.

— — — — — — — — — — — — — — — —

Dear Sander:

I came home early. You were
not home so I went upstairs to
Jannik's loft and fell asleep
on the daybed. I woke up and
went downstairs into the
kitchen. I heard laughter and
your voice, so I thought you
were on the phone. But you
weren't.

This is what I saw.

You were on the romper couch.
Your pants were on the floor.
Sitting next to you was Per
Larsen. Your eyes were closed.
His mouth was on your dick.
His head was bobbing up and
down. I felt faint. That's all.
I didn't feel angry. I didn't
want to kill anyone. All I

wanted to do was leave that
room and never come back.

So that's what I did, as you
both saw, and that's what I'll
do. You have killed my spirit.
You have killed my soul. You
have killed us.

I don't need any apologies, if
that's what you intend to do. I
don't know; maybe you don't
intend to do anything other
than to give what was most
precious to me--that happens
to be you--to somebody who at
one time would have never
even given you the time of
day. Well, I guess your dream
came true then. But my
nightmare has just begun.

I can never trust you again.
Ever. And without that trust,
what are we? Nothing at all.
But here's what your cruel
indiscretion did to us.

Besides putting an end to
what, until today, I thought
was perfect--obviously, I was
wrong, very wrong--I can now
no longer have a
relationship with your mama,
pop, sister, relatives, but
especially, Jannik. He loves
me, Sander, but how am I
supposed to keep the
relationship with him?

Am I supposed to make him
choose between you and me? Am
I supposed to act like all is
well, maybe have "visitation"
every other weekend? So I can
hear all about my family I no
longer have? So I can hear
how Per did this, and Per did
that? No, as much as it
absolutely murders my heart,
I refuse to subject that
wonderful boy, and myself, to
that kind of torture.

Did you think about how your
family will feel? I know them

well enough to know that
they will circle the wagons
around you, their wonderful
son. They are family, and I
expect nothing less from
those beautiful people whom I
love almost as much as I love
you. Oh, yes, <u>LOVE</u> you--not
LOVED, as in past tense.

If you think I'll get over you,
ever, think again.

Yes, I'm a survivor. I'm not
prone to rash thinking or
self defeating actions, or
even self harm. But I'm also
not someone who will stand by
and watch his life crumble in
front of him while his
supposed life-mate and best
friend sticks his cock into
somebody else's mouth. And
who knows what else you did,
or how often you did it,
before I saw it with my own
eyes?

This week my schedule will be
to take time from work as an
emergency. This qualifies, I
think.

Then I'll get an AIDS test.

Next, I will go shopping for a
new life. Do what you will
with my possessions. I don't
give a shit. Give them to the
Lutherans, or better yet,
burn it all. The cats are
yours. Everything is yours.
Keep the house.

I'm taking my car, and some
photos and my computer.
That's it. Just set the stuff
in my writing room and I'll
pick it up some night soon.
Ask Jannik to disassemble and
pack my computer. You'll
never know I was there; just
like you didn't know I was
there this morning.

To say you have hurt me is

beyond words. I understand that--hell, YOU understand that too, and I'm not going to berate you here. But I will say this: as much as you hurt me, you've hurt yourself twice as much.

You will never, never, _ever_ know anyone who loves you as much as I do.

You will <u>never</u> enjoy the kind of life we shared together, with anyone else, ever.

I will leave the Odense area and likely move near Copenhagen, because I don't want to chance an accidental meeting with any family or friends, and I especially don't want to run into you and Per shopping for china or dinnerware, or even for groceries! I couldn't take that.

So here's how I'm prepared to leave it.

I will contact the attorney and get a line on a good, fast divorce. As I said earlier, it's all yours.

I'll pay off the house note so you and Per can start fresh and free of debt. Which is what you'll need anyway, because he's never worked a day in his life that I can tell. I want you to keep the house because of Jannik's music studio. No reason that you should shake up his world any more than you already have.

I'll leave contact information with the attorney, but please only contact me in case of a true emergency; not because you want to make an end run at

saying you're sorry or
whatnot. (That's even if you
are sorry; maybe this is what
you wanted all along.)

I don't know what I did wrong,
or what I failed to provide
you emotionally,
financially, lovingly,
sexually, or anything else.
I'll admit I'm at a loss. But
there you go. We're not meant
to understand everything, or
maybe anything at all. One
thing's for sure; I don't
understand this, and I don't
understand you.

I love you. You mean
everything to me. I won't try
and "win you back" because
there's no way I could, even if
I was so inclined. Once you've
crossed the line as you have,
there's no turning back. So
who are we kidding?

I thank you for all of the

wonderful times we had. I
hope at least, from your point
of view, that they were good.
Maybe I've been in a fool's
paradise thinking one thing
while you felt another. I'll
never know, because no matter
what you say, I'll never be
able to trust you as before.

I wish you the very best, and
please don't paint a picture
that isn't true when you tell
people that we're no more.
Especially with Jannik and
Ingrid. <u>Tell the whole truth
of what you did.</u> I think you
owe me that much at least.
And please explain to Jannik
why his Johnnie Bond isn't
there anymore.

You created this mess, so you
have to own it. And after all
he's been through, and after
all we've shared as a family,
you owe him that much. I'm

counting on you to deliver on that request.

And lastly, I want you to consider that you just gave more ammunition to the homophobes—-ESPECIALLY MY FUCKING MOTHER—-and their stereotypical assumptions that all gays are promiscuous and go around sucking any dick that falls into their mouths.

You just gave them a chalk mark on their scoreboards of hate. Oh, and my mother's prayers were certainly answered, weren't they?! Thanks for that one, too, Sander.

I now see that life truly is a shit-pile that we are forced to claw through for the next meal, the next fuck, and the next chance to seek and secure some selfish goal.

I love you, Sander Lars
Hansen. I always will. I hope
you find happiness. And I
hope Per is worth it all.

Sex is an itch you just
scratch! But love? Sander,
that's the itch so far down
your back that you can't even
reach it with your own hand.
I hope for your sake that
Per's hand is long enough, but
I don't think so.

Sincerely,

Johnnie.

- - - - - - - - - - - - - - - - - - -

SANDER AND PER ARRIVED AT the Hansen
family home later in the day. Sander was
inconsolable; apoplectic. He didn't know what to do,
and Per wasn't any help at all. Was that surprising?
Not for Sander. He knew he'd fucked up badly,
perhaps permanently, and the devil who had
inspired it all was following him over to his parents'

house. Why? And why did he even care what Per did? What was he thinking? He was lost. Just... lost.

They arrived at the Hansen house and were greeted at the door by Jannik.

"Hey, Pokey. Where's Johnnie? Why's he here?" Jannik pointedly asked. Per caught the shift in the wind and did what Per does. He bugged out.

"I'll see you at practice, Sander. I'm for home now, so...yeah. See you." and he was gone, his car zipping around the corner before they'd shut the door.

"Is Mama here?" Sander asked.

"Yeah. So where's Johnnie?" Jannik pressed.

"He got back safe and sound, Spiderman. We'll see him soon. Can I have a private talk with Mama and Pop?" Sander said.

"I don't know how private it'll be. Ingrid's in there with her man," Jannik reported.

"Can you go upstairs for a bit? I promise it won't be too long, okay?"

"Yeah. Is everything okay?" Jannik asked.

"Sure. Now go on up, I'll talk with you soon."

Jannik traipsed up the stairs and Sander entered the living room. His face was drawn and he was doing his best to keep it together, but he was starting to crumble.

"Hi, guys." Sander began. All could clearly see that something was wrong. "Mama, Pop, can I talk with you for a minute?" His sister, Ingrid, and her boyfriend, Palle, graciously took the hint and moved to the kitchen. Sander stood in the center of the room like an errant schoolboy standing before the headmaster. Niels and Magda knew it was serious.

"Something really bad happened. And I don't know where to start. And I don't know what to do." That was it. Sander dissolved into tears. To his parents he became the little seven-year-old who'd hurt himself on the playground and was coming to them for comfort.

"What happened, son?" Niels asked. "What's wrong?"

"Pokey, tell us, yes?" Magda added.

"Johnnie left me and it's my fault! It's all my fault, and I don't know what to do about it! Oh, God, he's gone for good! For *good!*" Sander cried.

"What happened? Why's it your fault?" Magda pressed. "Son, you have to tell us!"

"Don't you see?! I was terrible to him! I was with Per and he saw us! He saw us, Mama! And then he left and he's never coming back!"

"What do you mean you were with Per? What does with mean? Were you with him at the movies?...

At a club? *What?*" Niels asked.

"I was with him! I was having sex with him! And Johnnie came home and saw us. He saw us!" Sander sobbed. He was borderline hysterical, something that Sander never was. Usually calm, collected, and unassumingly shy, Sander Lars Hansen was in the deepest throes of regret and despair like he'd never been before. But the worst was on the way.

"God fucking damn you! You fucking piece of dogshit! I'll fucking end you!" came the beyond angry shouts from Jannik as he tore into the room and made a beeline for his brother. He never slowed. He came at him full force and landed a striking blow on Sander's face.

Then he jumped him from behind and pulled him down by his neck, as wound up as a rattlesnake. He slugged him in the back of his head, hard. Then he quickly stood and started kicking Sander in his side, landing a glancing blow across his face just above his nose. Had he made contact, he'd have surely broken it.

Niels was on his feet, and Palle and Ingrid were running into the room. The immediate matter at hand was to end Jannik's attack. Sander was already bleeding from his ear, likely from the initial blow. And surprisingly, the young man refused to hit back.

He just let Jannik wail on him, and even when Palle grabbed him from behind the back, his hands interlocking beneath Jannik's chest, there was no stopping the force of the younger boy.

Ingrid ran back to the kitchen and returned with the gallon jug of ice water from the refrigerator. She waited for her opportunity but only ended up dousing her boyfriend and mama's new chair.

Jannik looked evil. Pure hatred coursed through his entire body and his last waterloo was to lift his legs while Palle held him and land a double pushing kick right into the small of Sander's back.

"Fuck you! Fuck you! *Fuck you, you fucking fuck!!!"* was all that Jannik could spit out. His brain was on overload, and after the stream of expletives landed, he just started crying and gave up the fight.

Niels picked him up and carried him to the bathroom while the others tended to Sander's cuts, and the bruises that were already appearing. What a shitty day it had become.

Jannik couldn't catch his breath, so Niels got the shower going, ice cold, and yanked his son's shirt off of him. He immediately dunked his head and shoulders under the solid stream, attempting to shock him back into reality. Niels was crying by now. He had never seen anything like this in his home, and knowing that the event was happening between two of the people he loved the most in the whole world was devastating to him.

"Okay, cowboy, how are you coming?" Niels managed to ask. "Feeling better a little bit?"

Jannik was still crying, but at least he was breathing steadily. He looked at his dad and nodded. His legs were shaking, a precursor to collapsing. He held tightly to his dad and looked pleadingly into his eyes.

"Papa, I'm so mad. I hate him! I hate him so much! Why did he do it, Papa?!" Jannik exclaimed.

"You don't hate anybody, sweet boy. You don't. Here, let's make the water a little warmer. Take your clothes off and let's just stay here for a bit, okay my son?" Niels said as soothingly as he could.

Jannik stripped off his pants and underwear and tossed them on the shower floor. Niels tested the water and removed the showerhead from its holder. This allowed him to spray the boy from every angle in a bid to make him feel better. It seemed to work.

Finally Jannik sat on the shower floor and let his daddy spray him while he tried to recover from the horrible events of that awful day. All he could think about was Johnnie. Where's Johnnie? Is he safe? Is he jumping off a bridge somewhere?

"Papa, what will we do about Johnnie? I'm afraid for him," Jannik said.

"I know son. I am too. We'll talk with Mama when everybody gets their wits back and we'll find him. You want to sit here for a while, son?" Niels asked kindly.

"Yes, Pop. I think I have to sit here."

"Here, give me your wet things and I'll be back with some pajamas in a little bit, yes?"

"Okay," Jannik agreed. "I'll be right here."

"Do you need anything?"

"I'm hungry. I really am, you know?" Jannik said.

"Okay, Mike Tyson, I'll bring you something back. You stay here and don't kill anybody while I'm gone."

Chapter 18

...AND THE NEXT

"COME OVER HERE, HANDSOME.

Come sit with me," Marge said, patting the sofa. "I have something for you, because you're my total soul gay."

"What?" I asked.

"Come here and I'll show you!" she grinned.

"This ain't one of them Gotta Buy Me Dinner First kinda offers, is it?" I joked. "Cuz I'm down to my last gay nerve, sister friend!"

"Get your yellow-haired tuckus over here," she ordered as I sat down beside her.

Long Before Morning

"What the hell is a tuckus?" I asked.

"You're sitting on it! And by all accounts it's a cute one," she chuckled. "Though I wouldn't know."

"Shut up, you greasy old Lezbo!"

"Ha! You'll have to do better than that, squirrel face! Now hush while I get all mushy and thoughtful on you. Listen to the old bag for a minute," she told me.

"Yes, ma'am."

"This is a poem. It's very, very special, and of everyone on this godforsaken planet you're the only one who I think might get it."

"Yeah?"

"Yeah. So sit there like the good boy that you are and listen, okay?" she said with such tender love in her voice.

"Okay. Go for it," I said. Then I leaned back on Marge's granny sofa (Really Marge? Scottish plaid with doilies?) and closed my eyes. She cleared her throat as she unfolded the pretty lilac stationery.

"The time was then, the time was
when... The time was yours, the time
was mine... It was our time, wouldn't
you agree?

"We had it good, we lived each day as if it were the last... We did for us, we did for all, and always did our best.

"And now the sun has set upon the things we used to have...

"We say the rain is something bad and what we do not want. But without the rain we'll never grow, together or apart; instead we'd stay the same...

"So, I will say, whatever comes, I'll cherish what we are... I promise that the time we had was never spent in vain...

"Yet one day, or night, or time that's yet to be... Whether sun or breeze or rain-a-pouring, the truth will come, Long before morning.

"We'll conquer the fear that sent us this warning; and this will come, Long before morning."

"Those are some very lovely words, Marge," I told her. "But they're a little too soon for me. I'm afraid it's a very long time until morning for this kid."

"I get it. Just keep it in your noggin for later, okay?" she said, patting me and petting me with such affection. Then it was time for crying jag number 42. She held me close and let me cry and didn't say a word. It wasn't necessary.

JANNIK CRIED HIMSELF TO SLEEP and woke the next day in a lot of pain. He wanted to do nothing more than to lie in bed and stare at the ceiling. He knew every crack, blemish, discoloration, and rough patch over his bed. He especially liked the little swab of paint that, when the light hit it in a certain way, looked like a clipper ship under full sail heading off to China for a load of tea. He wished he was aboard that ship, far away from yesterday's trauma.

Mama tapped lightly on the door.

"Enter if you dare!" Jannik called to her. He knew it was her because of the tentative knock. Pop never knocked; instead, he always said, *Hello!*

Anybody at home? through the door and waited for an invitation.

Ingrid would just do the universal knock: 1-2-3-4-5! She'd always done that.

And Sander never knocked because he had special privileges. He'd just walk in and say something like *Hey, asshole! How's your ass? Is it Holy?* Jannik would tell him not to address royalty in this way, and Sander would complete the bit with an exaggerated bow and the grand salutation, *Yes, Your Assholiness!*

None of that would happen today. If ever.

"How are you, Jan?" Mama asked him.

"Tired."

"I'll bet you are. Your brother wants to talk with you. Can he come in?"

"No. Never. I'm through with him," Jannik replied firmly. "And don't try to get me to go soft, because I won't."

"Okay. Maybe later," she said.

"Maybe never," Jannik promised. "Has anybody heard from Johnnie?"

"Not yet. But give it some time. He'll call you."

"I heard what he said; about what he did to Johnnie. I heard it from the stairs when he was telling you. He's a real asshole," Jannik declared.

"Yes, he made a very big mistake. But they'll work it out, don't you think?" Mama said. Mistake? *He made a mistake?* That was a bit of an understatement, Jannik thought. Washing whites with reds, or forgetting to turn on the dishwasher, or leaving the garden hose running—those were mistakes.

"He fucked up, Mama. No other way to say it. And I'm serious when I say I'm through with the guy. Johnnie's not coming back, and you know whose fault that is," Jannik reminded her.

"Okay. Well, you want to come down for some breakfast?" Mama asked.

"Is he down there?"

"Yes, I think so."

"Then no. I'll wait until it's gone," Jannik said with much disdain.

"I won't hear of you calling your brother an "It," do you understand?"

"I understand that I'm not gonna call it anything else. I want nothing more to do with it," Jannik sassed.

"Oh, you're just impossible! Fine! Stay up here in your little hate nest if you want to, but sooner or later you'll have to talk it out with your brother, whether you like it or not!"

"I don't like IT! I told you that," Jannik teased. "So get over IT."

"You're not too big to put over my knee," Mama smiled.

"I don't know... I did pretty good yesterday. I wouldn't mess around with me. I'm two-fisted!" Jannik smiled.

"Oh, be quiet! I'll see you later," Mama said, gently closing the door behind her. Then, through the door she casually mentioned that she'd be baking his favorite peanut butter cookies and a chocolate cake "just in case you decide to come down!"

"You're evil, Mother! You are a cold, hard, evil lady!"

––––––––––––––––––

TOWARD THE END OF THE WEEK Johnnie called to let the family know that he was alive, if not exactly well. He got Niels on the phone and asked him a favor: Would he move Johnnie's boat from its current mooring at the marina in Kerteminde over to Copenhagen?

Niels told him of course he would. Johnnie explained that he was planning to live aboard the forty-five-foot-long classic cabin cruiser until he could find a new house. He said he planned to let Sander have the home in Gelsted—he swore he never wanted to step foot in it ever again—and then buy a new place that was reasonably close to the American Embassy. Made sense, Niels thought. Johnnie always made sense.

What the hell was wrong with Sander? Niels pondered. The two were inseparable, and he knew that Johnnie practically worshiped his boy. And he assumed that Sander felt the same way about Johnnie.

The man was so kind, so loyal, and such a part of the family. He had brought Jannik back to them. And he was always so joyful; never was he in a bad or dark mood. Call it the Scandinavian way, but even Sander could go dark sometimes. He'd never seen his son lose his temper or become belligerent, but he had witnessed some pretty deep depression out of Sander. Johnnie seemed to be the key to keeping his son in a constantly positive state of mind. They were good together.

He recruited Jannik to be his shipmate for the four hour cruise to Copenhagen, and promised Johnnie that the boat would be safe and secure at its new berth in no more than forty-eight hours.

Johnnie thanked Niels profusely, and sounded like his usual, happy self as they ended the call. He noticed that not once did Johnnie mention or ask about Sander. Not even a hint, or a catch, or a false start that would indicate that he'd ever known his son or had been a very important part of Family Hansen. Things were different, and boy did it hurt.

Chapter 19

...AND THE ONE AFTER THAT

AFTER I SPENT THE WEEK AT MARGE'S

place I felt like it was time to put on my big boy pants and begin my life anew. Getting the boat delivered had been delayed a couple of days because of a windstorm that blew in off the Baltic. So I just stayed on with Marge until we could secure a date for the boat to arrive. She would arrive at the marina today.

The afternoon is so pretty. There's a gentle breeze, a little on the cool side, and it's a cotton ball puffy clouds day. An ice blue sky filled with happy birds; tiny wavelets in the harbor are disturbed by the occasional jumping fish coming up for a look-see. I look back, and then catch the stately lines of my

1929 cabin launch making her way slowly up the channel, Niels at the helm, and Jannik standing on the bow ready to toss me a mooring cable.

Jannik waved excitedly in my direction, and Niels expertly negotiated the turning basin and brought *Stargazer* starboard side to the dock. A textbook perfect docking. Niels throttled back to "Finish with Engine" and shut her down.

"Ahoy, mateys!" I called to them. Jannik secured the lines and the bumper fenders and ran straight for me, arms open as wide as he could. He threw his arms around me and hugged me for a good couple of minutes. I held his face against my chest and managed to pop a little kiss on the top of his head. Niels stepped off the vessel and hugged me as well.

"We miss you, Johnnie boy."

"I miss all of you. More than you can ever imagine," I told them. Jannik refused to let go, so I kind of unwrapped half of him from around me and stationed him off to my side. We buddy-walked down the dock and headed for some lunch. We'd get something and take it to the park and catch up on all the news.

NIELS AND JANNIK DECIDED to stay the night aboard *Stargazer* which I was happy to accommodate. I needed the company, and Jannik needed to be with me. I think Niels was just excited to be out of the house for awhile.

"I'm so sorry for what Sander pulled," Niels said. "I don't know what got into him. It's just not like him at all."

Jannik's face was stone cold at the mention of his brother. He added, "He's a big turd and I've flushed him in the toilet!" He looked at his dad, expecting some sort of censure. None came. Niels just shrugged and took a bite of his pølse—that wonderful Danish sausage. I remember when I saw Sander selling pølser outside the train station in Odense. *Damn it! Stop that!*

Niels said that he finally decided to finish Mama's new washing machine room. "Now that the weather is so lovely, I've run out of excuses. It's almost finished, anyway. I don't know why it takes me so long."

Jannik said, "It's because of that big thing you sit on."

"What thing?"

"Your lazy ass!"

The laughter came easily enough, and it was like

old times. And that was the problem. These two beautiful people were a direct link to the life I was leaving. I didn't want to leave it, either. And I admit I'd go weak in the knees about my resolve about every two hours. But I could never trust him again. There was just nothing he could say.

We did all the usual boy things together. We told dirty jokes—Jannik was the king of those, for sure. I let Niels go on and on about sports scores or teams or jockstraps, or whatever-the-fuck he was going on about. The only thing I know about sports is that the guys look cute in their uniforms. Especially the swimmers.

We even made it to Jannik's earthquake movie that he wanted to see so badly. It was really good. The only bad part was when I instinctively turned to my right when a really cool thing happened in the film. See, I swung my head to my right expecting to meet Sander's eyes. He would have snapped his head to his left so we could trade a quick, knowing smile about how awesome that moment of the movie had been. But he wasn't there.

Jannik knew.

He looked up at me and he just knew. He took my left hand in his and gave it a quick squeeze. *I know what just happened, Johnnie. I'm so sorry for what*

266

my brother did. I love you. He conveyed that soothing message in a singular squeeze of his hand on mine, and offered a tentative smile. Then we went back to watching Los Angeles fall into the sea. I'll bet Dwayne 'The Rock' Johnson would kick Sander's ass for me if I asked him to.

───────────────

"Pop, jeg er nødt til at bo her med Johnnie for et stykke tid," Jannik told his dad, as we walked back to the boat. *"Han ved det ikke, men han har brug for nogen til at være sammen med ham!"*

I said, "Jannik, you *do* know that I both speak and understand Danish, right?" Niels laughed. "And I'll be just fine. But if you want to stay with me you're more than welcome to as long as Pop says it's okay."

"Oh, God, yes! Keep him!" Niels joked. Jannik delivered a good-natured slug to his arm, and Niels playfully recoiled. "No! Not that! I saw in my living room what you can do, Slugger Hansen!"

"So can I stay with you?"

"Of course. But you have to swab the deck, walk the plank, and let me call you Gilligan," I said.

"Okay. I can do these things. What's Gilligan?"

"You don't have a clue! I like that!" I teased.

Niels would stay the night and head back to Odense by train in the morning, no doubt rendering an up-to-the-second text report to Mama. She was probably standing at the kitchen window right then, with her ear trained towards Copenhagen, hoping to pick up some valuable intelligence on the state of a one Johnnie Allen. I should have recruited her to my bosses at work.

"Johnnie, will you hear me for a minute?" Niels asked in his shy way. Of course I would. "Listen. I think Sander is an idiot. Thing is, he knows he is, too. I had a long talk with him before we left for the boat and he's so sorry. He admits everything he did, and wants to apologize to you and he doesn't want to separate. Can you talk with him?"

"I just can't," I said. "And it's not because I don't love him. I do. And it's not because I haven't forgiven him, because I already have, Pop."

"Then if you've forgiven him, why won't you talk to him?"

"Because I can't trust him. I can never, ever trust him, and that's the hardest thing," I told him. "And that's the thing that hurts the most, because the one thing...the *one big thing* that we had over every other couple on earth was that trust," I explained. "Love, attraction, friendship, sex, those are all part of it. But it was our trust in each other that was the glue. At least I thought so."

"I understand, son, I do. But you know, me and old Magda have hit the rocks a couple times but we always bounced back. None of us is perfect, and Lord knows she has a million reasons to kick me to the curb every day, but she doesn't."

"Have you ever walked in her having sex with your neighbor, or any of her old boyfriends?" Niels went silent. "That little dick you used to see when you changed his diapers, and that little butt you used to wipe was stuck inside a guy who hated and despised your boy all through school. They were laughing together, Pop. They were moaning and laughing and going at it full bore, and I guess it woke me to the fact that there wasn't as much there with us as I must have thought there was. And it kills me."

Niels just nodded. He'd tried, but he knew. "Will we not see you anymore, Johnnie?" He was crying now. The last time I'd seen tears in that strong man's eyes was at our wedding. "Please say that we can still see you. We all love you so much, and you're just as much a part of the Hansens as any of us."

"Of course I want to always see you. But what happens when he comes home with Per, or some other guy down the road? You'll have to treat him like you have with me. Sander will want you to love his new man just as much, so how will you be able to do that with me still in the picture?" I asked him. "And what about Jannik?"

"Yes. That's the biggest problem of all. You see, he told us he will have nothing to do with his brother ever again. He won't even say his name. He is so dark and angry; Magda and me have never seen the little guy like this. We none of us thought he had it in him to be so hateful," Niels said. "Everything's just so fucked up right now we don't know what way to look!"

"I know it. Boy, don't I know it." was all I could manage.

"What about your job? Will you stay in Denmark?"

"Yeah. I mean, it's not Denmark's fault that your kid's an asshole," I chuckled. Niels joined in on the laugh, which was good for both of us. "Besides, I'm stuck for three more years anyway before I could even request a move."

"Thanks, Obama!" Niels joked.

Jannik popped out of the forward hatch like a whack-a-mole and let us know that *Denmark's Got Talent* was coming on the T.V. He promised us popcorn and sodas and all kinds of good things, so we ducked into the cabin to enjoy the evening together before Niels went home and everything changed.

Chapter 20

...AND YET ANOTHER WEEK

THIS WAS THE WEEK OF CHANGE. IT

was time to file with the court. Dissolution of Marriage: Form Nr. AA-04. Non contested dissolution—no custody, closed hearing, please date here. So simple. Sign a form; sign away your life. We can do it in the lawyer's office; no need to see a judge. In thirty days it'll be like it never happened.

Some things are just too easy.

Long Before Morning

SANDER TRIED TO GET HOLD of me to try and keep us together, but I was having none of it.

He tried through Mama, Ingrid, (not Jannik), and even, of all people, Per Larsen. Yep! I got a voicemail from Per admitting that it was all his fault, that he had tricked Sander into doing it, that he and Sander would never see each other again, *bla bla bla.*

Jannik hadn't softened one tiny bit regarding his brother. Sander had also launched a campaign to win him back, but it had fizzled like a wet bottle rocket.

So here we were. Over, said, and done.

When I close my eyes, I see him.

When I open my eyes, I see him.

In the shower? See him.

On the street? See him.

In Jannik's face? I see him. (Genetics, more than anything!)

You get my drift.

So what's a boy to do? I miss my life. I miss everything we'd built together. Shit! Shit! Shit! Shit! Fucking shit! Why did you do it?! If I could just get my head around *why!*

THE DAYS JUST MERGE. ONE DAY, is just another day, is just another fucking day.

It's been a week since Niels and Jannik were here. I spend my days on the boat and, of all places? . . . *Fucking Facebook*. God, what a loser's life. Checking on statuses! Yay! Handholding distant strangers through their own shit. Oh, how nice of you, Johnnie. You're world's falling apart and you're little mister helper boy scout. Your whole life you've done this, and what has it gotten you? Even your mother hates you, Johnnie. Remember that scathing, shit-filled letter that she wrote you earlier in the summer? Well, fellas, my shit's worse than yours.

Like if I'm cute!   I gonna hit a bitch!   I'm so depressed! I'm gonna cut myself!!! Look at me, me, me! I hate my parents-school-life-hair-dick!

Fuck off, you little turds!

Rate me for a tbh! The Confederate flag is part of my heritage! Like if you agree! Obama is the devil! I'm gonna delete half of my friends list!

Do it, you little fuck! You want problems? I'd gladly export some of mine to your whiney, privileged, idiot ass. BTW, you're not cute, your bathroom mirror selfies are vomit inducing, you can't spell, and your breath stinks! (I just have to assume that last one.)

Long Before Morning

What the hell! I'm yelling at a Facebook page. Sander Lars Hansen, this is all your fault! But is it? What did I do? I must have done something! He doesn't love me anymore. That would have to be it, because why else would he have sex with that brainless moron bully who is worth less than... Well, he must be worth more than me because he's the one who had Sander's cock in his mouth. Right?

I've got to get out of here. Maybe I'll just walk to town. Maybe there's a concert, or a club. Maybe I'll luck out and a bus will hit me.

I put on long pants and a nice shirt. My cool leather jacket that always turns heads. (Sander calls it my Indiana Jones jacket. It's brown and it really smells good. He told me it's his favorite jacket that I wear.)

There's music playing. There's about ten nightclubs in a two block strip and I just might go to every one of them. That's stupid. Why would I do that? Okay, three of them are gay clubs so I'll pick one or all of those.

I choose Bottoms Up, the one out of the three that has a real band playing, not just that thumpa thumpa thumpa thumpa stuff that's cool when you're on the prowl for dick or ass, but not when you're in the mood to jump off a building. Which is out of the question because the tallest building here is only six stories high. The survivability statistics lean toward life as a vegetable instead of certain death. Best I hang with the older crowd and hear live, local indie tunes presented by Nathalia and the Nats. Who knows, maybe they're a folkie drag act.

There's nothing like a good, draft-poured Danish beer with greasy chicken wings and French fries. There's also something to be had for watching older guys totally undress you with their bloodshot eyes when your ego's taken the ultimate hit. I think seeing Sander's cock being slurped by The Larsen qualifies.

"What're you drinking?" the fifty-something asks me, not even bothering to hide his wedding ring.

I answered, "Beer. Odense Pilsner. Are you taking a poll? Like, *In a Gallup Poll, blond American guys prefer pilsner over ale twelve to one?*"

"Ah! You're American! That answers the question!"

"What question?"

"Why you're so good looking. I noticed you when you came into the bar," he said. What a bunch of bullshit. "Can I buy you another?"

"Sure. Why not?" I said. He went to the bar so fast I thought he was going to turn a table over with his legs as he bumped past. The music started up and

Long Before Morning

I figured I'd just sit back, enjoy the night, completely frustrate the old dude—passive aggressive, I know—and then go home when the boredom meter climbed to ten.

The guy brought some beers back and set them on the shaky little table. "Here you go, cutie. What's your name? I'm Randy."

"Hey, Randy. I'm Paul," I told him. Well, it's my middle name! What good are they if you won't haul 'em out and use 'em every so often. Then he said some stupid shit.

"Hey! That's funny! I'm Randy, you're Paul! Randy Paul! Get it? We could be president! Randy Paul!"

Kill me now. Just do it. Maybe I'll be lucky and I'll let him take me home and he can kill me there. He could be one of those crazy, mad-ass killers and I could be, like, victim number thirty-six. He could chop off my head and put it in his fridge with all the other heads, and my troubles would end. Then my story could be co-opted into an episode of next season's *Law and Order: SVU*.

Hell, I'd even let him rape me first as long as he'd promise to kill me after.

"Wow! A sense of humor and everything! Where are you from?" I asked.

"Toronto. That's in Canada!" he informed me.

"Hey! I've heard of Canada before! Wow! All the way over here! What're you doing in Copenhagen?" I ventured.

"Talking to the cutest and coolest guy in the whole world, that's what. What about you? You here on vacation?" he charmed. Oh, what a Lothario he was! My knickers were shivering in anticipation of the one blessed day that I might see him in his all his gray-haired nakedness.

I replied, "No, I live here. I work at the U.S. Embassy, and I got posted up here to the Great White North." Then I dropped the bomb. "So who's the ring for?"

"The ring?"

"The ring."

"I don't get...the ring?" he said. Ha! He'd forgotten to take it off!

"Who do I look like? Frodo, or something? I don't do rings," I said, pointing straight at his gold band.

"Oh, that!" he grinned sheepishly. "That's just my..."

"Save it."

"No really! It's a ring that I usually wear on another finger but it doesn't fit anymore," he lied.

279

"Uh huh... Can I see your phone?" I asked him.

"Why?" he said, handing it over to me. God, he really must want sex badly. See, this is what they mean when they say 'Thinking With Your Dick'. In two presses of the buttons, just two little click-clicks, and there on the screen was a nice, Olan Mills Photography pic—probably taken at the Wal-Mart photo center, or at Dillard's—of the Randy family all dressed up in their Easter best.

There they were: Randy, Mrs. Randy, Randy Junior, Young Master Randy, and little Randette. Smiling to beat all, they looked like refugees from the *America's Funniest Home Videos* studio audience.

"Friends of yours?" I asked. "Nice looking people, Randy. They back at the hotel? Did you guys see Tivoli yet? Bet the kids loved it." he took the phone from my hand and, believe it or not, I think he actually felt bad. "Go home, Randy."

He stood to leave, nervously, and he did the funniest thing that actually made the whole exchange laughable. As he got up he grabbed one of my chicken wings and started eating it.

"Dude!"

"Oh my goodness! Paul, I'm so sorry! I just... When I'm nervous I eat, and I just... Here, I'll buy you another basket of--"

"No problem, Randy. Seriously. Just go hug your kids and we'll forget the whole thing," I told him. We actually traded smiles and we parted with no hard feelings. What a night! Oh, you think it's over? Ha! Jokes on you!

———————————————

I NURSED BOTH OF MY BEERS to the bottom of the bottles and really had a good time listening to The Nats. I'd go see them again. I bet Sander would really like that song she sang---

I remember that movie when you could get your memories erased. Specific ones. I wonder what I'd do if that was truly possible? Would I erase all knowledge of Sander Lars Hansen? Or would I just erase that awful day in my living room when I saw *His Cock in Per Larsen's Fucking Big Mouth?!*

I don't know. Too much to think about. It was time to head back to the boat anyway.

By the way, just to let you know, I purposely eliminated the five other attempts on my penis these last three hours at the bar. Oh well. What can you expect when you walk into a place called Bottoms Up? I give the old mutts credit for trying. Doubt, if I

281

were them, that I'd have the balls. But then again, my plan was to have gray hair with Sander by my side, and me next to him. Sander. You fucking idiot. Sander. I love you so fucking much.

I left the noisy warmth of the club and walked into the cooling night. I love the streets of Copenhagen. The narrowness. The wonderful smells—coffee, bakery goods, fireplaces, the aroma of different cuisines drifting out of the opened windows of apartments up and down the block.

A taxi was parked in the bike lane, probably waiting for drunks to stumble out of the bars. He would hit them up, and they'd take the offer. They would arrive home safely, and he would be the richer for it. He saw I was walking straight and with purpose, so he didn't waste his pitch on me. He bid me a good evening and went back to puffing on his cigar. Now I could add that to the collection of smells on this odd night.

A car sped past. A rental, based on the Hertz #1 Club sticker on the boot, it was crammed with a likely crew of drunken tourists probably on the prowl for hookers. I wanted to shout, *Two streets over, you jerks,* but then why should I help them get their dicks wet?

I hate dangerous drivers. I know a little something about what a vehicle is capable of, and it burns me to see a bunch of Brats in a Beamer go screaming by in a street with so many blind intersections and filled with people—like me!

Then, about halfway up the next block, the BMW screeched to a halt. A guy got out of the car and started running toward me. I mean directly. A beeline; absolutely sure of it.

"Hey! Stop!" the man shouted. What the fuck was this?

I ducked into an alley and was determined to avoid this numb nuts with a passion. I was in no mood for a drunk Brit. Not tonight.

He saw me, though, and adjusted his route accordingly. Okay, time for some tradecraft.

I skirted into an impress in the side of the old building and waited for him to pass. I clearly heard the running footsteps growing closer, then the skid of his shoes when he turned into the alley. I stayed put. I knew he'd either keep running or backtrack. In either case, he wouldn't see me.

"Johnnie! You down here? Johnnie Allen!"

What in the hell? Yes, the voice was definitely English. As in from England. Was it one of the lads from the Ops team? I held back, but I did allow myself a quick recon peek. Out. Lean back. Nothing. Just a dark figure about fifty meters away. His back is to me. This was very unsettling, to say the least.

He turned and began walking back towards my position. Again, he wouldn't be able to see me. But now I wanted to see him. Who the hell was stalking me—extremely vigorously, I might add—here in downtown Copenhagen at two in the morning on a night when I, myself, didn't even know I'd be here?

Alright. Time to take the upper hand because this wasn't going to fly for me. I was fed up.

I quietly removed my work phone and prepared it for the next step. I counted his steps, listening intently as they got closer. When his shoes scraped across some gravel I had noticed on the ground before I took cover, I literally jumped in front of him while simultaneously triggering the rescue strobe light on my phone.

"Down on the ground, now! On your knees! I'm not fucking around!" I screamed in my evil mean scary voice. It worked. He was blinded, confused, and dropped backwards onto his ass. I switched the strobe to halogen flashlight mode and lit up that whole alley. What I saw was the frightened, terrified face of...

"Johnnie! Don't shoot! It's Thom! Fucking hell, mate, it's Thom!!!"

"What the...?" I stammered.

"Thom! Thom Bleaker! We met aboard *HMS Vigilant*! Please, mate!"

Damn, I'd scared the man to death. And damn if it wasn't my awesome friend, Petty Officer Thom Bleaker, Royal Navy, probably sitting in his own shit after that performance I'd made.

"Oh, God! Thom! I'm so sorry! Let me help you!" I felt so bad. You cannot imagine how rotten I felt. This was one of the kindest, most considerate people I had ever met, and I was ready to clean his clock.

"Whew! It's you. Damn, remind me to call ahead next time," he said as he struggled to his feet. I'd really shaken him up.

"What are you doing here? I mean, how'd you know I was here?" I managed to ask as he dusted himself off best he could. I could see a tear in the nice slacks he was wearing. I just couldn't believe the whole thing.

"I didn't. *Vigilant* is at the naval base across the canal, and I've got two days leave. We all pitched in for a hire car and we were just looking for a place for a late drink, you know? And I just looked out the car and there you were true as can be," he explained. "I told me mates to pull off, and then got out and called after you. You know the rest," he smiled.

"I can't believe it! This is great! Can you hang with me for a bit?" I asked him, grinning ear to ear.

He said, "Long as you like! I don't have to report back until 1800 hours day after next. You guys live round here?"

"Believe it or not, you're not the only one living on a boat these days! I have a cabin cruiser I'm staying on at the marina. Fancy a look?" I asked him.

"Lead the way, Skipper!"

"What about your mates?" I asked.

"No worries. Doubtful we'd have stayed together before night's end, anyways. Let's see this yacht of yours!"

We headed for *Stargazer's* mooring and right away started catching up since the last time we'd seen each other. It was about a year ago. I had been given a no notice assignment called Operation Watercress. I had seventy-two hours to design and execute the exfiltration of the British consul and his family out of Morocco.

The primary vehicle for the exfil was a British submarine, *HMS Vigilant*. Thom and I shared his quarters and we got to know each other quite well in that short time. He learned that I was gay and was engaged to Sander, and I found out that he was gay when he told me that he was kind of crushing on me. Nothing physical happened between us, of course. But I remembered thinking that if I wasn't already spoken for I'd have definitely had him over for a cup of tea. And maybe crumpets?

"Look. That's her there," I told him, pointing out my sweet baby gently rolling with the dock. We headed down the gangway from the esplanade to the floating pier and stepped aboard the boat.

"Oh, she's a right dandy, she is. Beautiful, mate. Just beautiful," Thom said. "Hey, should you have called your fella and told him you were bringing an old navy shipmate home with you?"

"Yeah. About that. Come in and have a seat. I'll catch you up," I said.

"BLIMEY! YOU COULD TOSS ME with a feather," Thom said. "So sorry, mate. You must be gutted."

"Yeah. Good way to put it. I could imagine me doing that to him before I'd ever think it was possible for him to do it, you know?" I said.

"I do. I mean, I know from first hand that you'd never cheat on him like that. And you really walked in on him just like that?" Thom asked.

"I did. They didn't know I'd gotten home early and was upstairs asleep. I came down and there they both were," I explained.

"And you just left? Didn't say a word?"

"Uh huh. I took my car and drove to the parking lot of the apartment I used to live in because I knew nobody would bug me, and I cried my eyes out."

Thom gently put his arm around me, consoling me. "I'm so sorry, mate."

"When I'd finished the crying jag, I wrote him the letter of all letters telling him just how it was gonna be and I drove all the way back to Gelsted and tossed it on the dashboard of his car. The car I paid for, by the way. Fuckin' Dane!" I told him.

"The Dane of Pain!" Thom added. I let out a big laugh. You gotta love gallows humor. I engage in it at every opportunity, and it just struck me funny.

"He spanked this Yank!" I added.

"That he did, mate. Oh, I'm not laughing at you. You know that, right?" he said, exploding with laughter.

"You Brit Twit!" I said, and that just made him laugh even more. "So you're staying with me until it's time for you to report back aboard, right?"

"Okay, you fey gay!"

Chapter 21

LOST AND BROKEN

I T'S TIME FOR BED NOW. THOM'S IN THE

forward cabin, and I'm in the Master's cabin, aft.

So as you can guess, I'm in quite the quandary. Though most wouldn't see it that way.

There is a gorgeous man less than thirty feet away from me. All I would have to do is say, "Thom."

He wouldn't hesitate for a moment. He'd be lying right beside me, bidding me to do whatever I wish to him sexually.

Long Before Morning

Fancy a blow job, Thom? No problem. Wanna fuck me in the ass? Let me spread these cheeks for ya, mate! Wanna cum on my face? Sure! How about you eat out my ass? Sure, a whole hour's fine with me! That'll get me all ready for the ass plowing you're about to give me. And yes, Thom, your balls are simply the best.

But I lie here alone thinking instead of He who should not be named.

I could have sex with Thom—believe me, I have the right to it; I earned it the hard way—and I can pretend it's Sander. Kind of ease into the single life. I mean, I hear it's not healthy to give up heroin cold turkey. They wean them off the drug. It must be the same when you and your man break up because you walked in on him *getting his cock sucked by Per Fucking Larsen!* Don't I get the same consideration as a junkie? Can't I get weaned off of Sander?

I guess I could just jack off. I've got enough mind porn locked up in there to last me till I need the Viagra boost in about fifty years! (It'd *better* be fifty years!) Hell, I could even jack off to Thom. I got enough furtive looks at him on the submarine, and tonight I snapped a mental image of his massive—and I do mean *massive*—bulge swimming in his trousers.

I could do. But I won't. Instead I retreat into this depressive slumber I've come to know. I'll rejoin the misery in the morning. Goodnight.

"HELLO, THIS IS JOHNNIE. If you know your party's extension, please press sixty-nine! This call may be recorded for later phone sex! By the way, this week's <u>six</u> winning lotto numbers are five-three-eleventy—" BEEEEP!

"Hi, uh, yeah... This is Pokey—I'm means Sander. Uhmm, I speaking the English for you because you shall hear this in your language, yes? Because this you are deserving.

"I am worse human in all the world, Johnnie. I am so very sorry for this what I do to you. It not is no one fault except for me, you know? Not is Per's because I am man who making his own decision and I am one who have make this very bad thing for us.

"Johnnie, please. I never shall ever do this ever. I will say also I love no one ever more. I wish to promise this; if you not are take me back, then I shall stay with my mother and father and just stay alone. I

293

not have deserve such as you in the first place, and I never do again.

"Can you know how much you meaning to me? But that not important. As I say, I not am—" BEEEEP!

"Hello again, I'm sorry I runs out of room on the machine. You see, I am so selfish to do what I do. I cannot explain except for in first time I have over Per Larsen. He have make my school time very not so good. And he come to me and I buys his bullshit.

"All I can say is for to asks if there is mercy in for me in your heart, Johnnie. I know your heart. It is much bigger than all the world and I make my hands together like in the church and say please will you love me again? Well, if you can, I am here. If you must not then I understand for you. I love you. I never not will love you, Johnnie. Okay, it is Sander. Good-bye."

"JANNIK, WE HAVE TO HAVE A TALK with you right now because you're going to have to be a man, and you're going to have to be one now," Mama said as the boy walked into the kitchen to window shop at the refrigerator door.

"Do we have any orange juice?" he asked.

"Jan, please respect your mother better than that. You're starting to cross some lines we don't appreciate, and you're not like this. Come sit with us," Pop said. The boy shut the fridge and settled instead for a bottle of lemon soda and a box of Cheese Nips he grabbed off the counter. He sat across from them; not unpleasant, but clearly guarded.

"You know there are changes coming," Mama began. "And we don't like them. But they're here. They're knocking on the door and they're here."

"So don't answer the door," Jannik reasoned.

Pop said, "Don't be Mister Smart Nose! We've got a problem and we have to face it, and we need your help."

"I'm not being a smart nose! He screwed everything up, so why is it our problem?" Jannik asked. "I'm sick of that all the world stops because he causes this awful trouble."

"Here's why it's our problem, Jan. It's because he's part of this family, just like you are. We know he messed up. He knows he did. And it's up to Johnnie whether or not they are together. But right now they're not, so your brother's moving back here for a while," Pop said.

"What?! For how long?!" Jannik exclaimed in disbelief. He felt totally betrayed by his parents. "You can't do that! *I live here!*"

"We can do that. And he'll be here until he gets his act together," Mama added.

"Oh! So forever, then! Mama, he's an idiot!"

"Perhaps so. But he's our idiot. And that makes him your idiot, too! And no idiot of ours gets turned away at that door for any reason, Jan. Ever!" Pop declared.

"Then I'll move. I will not live with that asshole, because there's something you don't know!" Jan argued. "Johnnie's not the only one who walked in on those two bastards acting like apes in a jungle!"

Pop and Mama exchanged glances. It hit Mama first. "Ohhh...*shit!*"

"What, Mags?" Pop asked with concern. She met his eyes but he was still confused.

"Before all this happened? When those two were at each others' throats? Remember when I had to pick Jan up at the boys'?" Mama reminded him. Then it hit Pop like a brick wagon.

"What'd you see, son?"

"Put it this way, it was worse than what Johnnie saw. So we finally had it out and he swore me to secrecy and I said fine, but only if he never, ever did anything like that to Johnnie ever again." Jannik began sobbing.

"But he did, Mama. He did it again, and this time Johnnie saw it, and it broke Johnnie's heart! Pop, you saw Johnnie in Copenhagen! He's broken forever over this, and I can't do anything to make it better, and here you are both bringing him here and I hate him! *I hate him!*" Jannik cried. This would take a while, the parents knew.

Pop rose up and pulled Jannik away from the table in his chair. He leaned down and picked his baby boy up and took him in a bear hug, secured in his burly arms. They walked to Pop's chair and he sat down, Jannik still in his arms, and reclined so the saddened youngster could lie across his daddy and fall asleep.

Pop couldn't make the hurt go away, but he made the hurt feel better, and that's all that a daddy could do.

Long Before Morning

THE MORNING SUN STREAMED into the forward porthole of Thom's cabin aboard *Stargazer*. He felt the warmth on his face before he ventured to open his eyes.

Fully awake now, he felt completely recharged. He also felt secure, at home even, aboard his friend's cabin cruiser. How could this be coincidence? Certainly the universe wasn't so cruel that it would engineer such a chance meeting with someone he'd never forgotten, in a place that until two weeks before the man had never lived?

He couldn't stop thinking about the gorgeous blond man in the next cabin. What it must be like to hold him, squeeze him, to make love to him. He'd caught a glimpse of him from behind back aboard *HMS Vigilant* when Johnnie changed his underwear in their shared quarters. He'd had a perfect view of his ass, and his large balls hanging there like a pair of apples on Eve's tree. And just as forbidden, he lamented.

He threw on his clothes and entered the galley and saloon. Johnnie sure kept his craft shipshape, Thom noticed. No small compliment coming from a Royal Navy petty officer.

Thom sussed out the coffee maker and got a pot brewing for the two of them, and loaded up the toaster with what appeared to be some rather tasty looking bread.

Opening the fridge revealed all kinds of good things—jams, jellies, milk, butter, creamed cheese. And there was a rasher of bacon all cooked up, and a large bowl of strawberries. Jackpot!

He zapped the bacon in the microwave, and scooped little bowls of strawberries topping them with whipped cream. Fit for an admiral, he thought. And to him, Johnnie was nothing less than that.

Thom was fascinated by Johnnie's job, of course, and he thought the man was nothing short of physically perfect. A king's ransom, he thought of Johnnie's sleek, sporty form. All of that was good, but it was his personality that attracted him the most.

Johnnie was funny, smart, interested in Thom's life, and above all he was loyal. Thom had just assumed that night on the submarine that, offered a roll in the hay, Johnnie would agree and they'd have some fun, awesome, sloppy, casual sex. He wouldn't say anything, and he'd assume that Johnnie wouldn't tell his man. Boys will be boys.

But Johnnie wasn't like that. And when he deflected Thom's advances he did it in such a kind and considerate way, even tossing in what to him must have been a casual compliment, but to Thom meant the world. He'd never been turned down before, and not felt bad about it. But with Johnnie, he didn't feel bad at all. He didn't even feel the least bit embarrassed by it.

And now he was aboard the man's beautiful boat making a tip-top breakfast that the two gay men would soon be enjoying together. Could something possibly be happening for the both of them? Thom told himself that if there was, he would wait for Johnnie as long as he needed to. In fact, he would insist they take it slow, he decided. The last thing he wanted was to be the rebound relationship for a man who was still very much in love with the one who had wronged him so.

The microwave beeped signaling that the bacon was ready, and he was flicking the last dollops of whipped cream onto the strawberries. The toast was ready, and it was time to eat. Once everything was on the table, Thom tapped quietly on Johnnie's cabin door.

I LAID THERE FOR AT LEAST HALF an hour just listening to Thom work in the galley. I figured a navy man like Thom would have everything in hand, and it was nice seeing somebody else take care of something for once. You have no idea how good bacon smells on a gorgeous morning inside the wooden cabin of a classic cruiser.

Thom was fussing with the last details, I could tell, and the next thing I heard were his taps on my door.

"Come, galley slave!" I joked. He peeked his head around the door and smiled warmly.

"Morning, Skipper! Breakfast is ready in the main saloon. E-deck, starboard side, table twelve. Sir. Cute cabin boy reporting. Sir."

"That the shit you say to Captain Madge?" I asked playfully.

"I wish! That man's a god!" Thom laughed. "I'd be his cabin boy any day! Come on, mate, grub for your gob!"

"On my way!"

Thom did an outstanding job with breakfast. He obviously wanted to make an impression, and I didn't withhold the praise he so deserved. It was awesome, and he'd made it from bits and pieces I'd picked up from the fruit market, the baker's, and Jannik's multiple trips to Brugsen's Supermarket.

"Damn, Thom, jump that nuclear rustbucket you're on and be my personal steward! This is great, man!" I told him. Seriously, it was fantastic.

"Don't tempt me, mate. Believe me, I would," Thom replied.

I teased him, "What if I say, *Hi sailor!* Will that help any?"

"Oh, now you're playing dirty!" he smiled, reaching for the boysenberry jam. "Keep it up and you'll have a loyal crewman forever. We'll just look over our shoulders for Her Majesty's Royal Military Police and dodge those buggers for all our days, but you're worth it!"

"Wow! I'm honored, Thom. But I hope you're kidding. Those guys are pretty intense," I said. Thing was, I got the feeling he was serious. If I had asked him to do it, I think he'd have found a way.

Chapter 22

JANNIK'S HAD ENOUGH

I WAS WONDERING IF I SHOULD MAYBE

mention what finally, uh, transpired between Thom and me. I think it's only fair, because if I didn't the readers of this journal would undoubtedly form their own conclusions anyway. So in the interest of full disclosure, as well as prurient interest (look it up!), against my better judgment I've decided to describe it here.

First, put your eyes back into your head. Just listen.

To say that I wasn't attracted to Thom would be an obvious falsehood. He is a beautiful man, inside and out. But at the time I reconnected with him, as you already know, I found myself in the throes of deep depression and confusion over Sander.

I love Sander. I always will. I just can't be with him anymore because I can never trust him again.

But I am young, male, sexually uninhibited, and of course very lonely. This is the perfect formula for the dreaded rebound relationship. This I do not want. But yesterday I very much wanted to be with someone that I care for. Like Thom.

But I also wanted to preserve, for a while anyway, what I have or had with Sander.

So now I'll take you there . . .

"Can I ask you something? Honestly?" Thom began. "And if you can't answer honestly, it's perfectly okay if you say so."

"You want to ask me if I want to have mad homo sex with you, right?" I replied. "Honest enough for you?"

"You dick! You're awesome!" he laughed. "Seriously, I was gonna ask you that, mate!"

"Well the answer to that is yes, I would very much like to. I think you're an amazing man, Thom. But I just can't. Not yet, anyway," I explained. I saw his face fall just a bit, and I can't tell you how difficult it was for me to take the high road on this one. And part of me wanted to knock me upside the head for it.

"But I have an idea if you're willing, Thom," I said.

"What's that?"

"Could we go in my cabin to the large bed, get completely starkers, and have a wank together? I mean, it's not the whole shebang, I know. But I think it's fair to all concerned, and I'd enjoy being with you in that way.

"I mean, it'd be just like at one of your snobby English boys' schools where all the lads lay around and wank the day away!" I told him with a huge grin plastered across my mug. "Yeah?"

"Fucking right, yeah!" he chuckled.

We headed to my cabin and watched each other undress. There was no hesitation; we just stripped off and climbed onto the bed. I wanted to do the very best I could allow myself to do for him, and made sure he had a good view of me all the way around as I took up my side of the bed.

Thom laid right beside me, a little lower down the bed so he could kind of rest his head in the little crook between my left shoulder and the side of my neck. His hair felt nice, and he was already rock hard when I glanced down to check him out.

Nearly eight inches, I'd guess, and very fat, his cock was as impressive as I'd imagined it to be. You have no idea the self control that it took to not go for it, mouth and throat wide open. If I had have done, this would be an entirely different report.

He fixed his eyes on me, and seemed very taken by what I had down there. He rose up and got nearer to it, and then I immediately figured out why: mine was the first cock he'd ever seen up close that was circumcised.

"So that's one, is it? Got the old razor snip when you was a youngster, eh? Must of hurt like a motherfuck," he said.

"Well, I was a baby so fortunately I have no recollection of the actual mutilation taking place. But it was definitely a motherfuck. That bitch really fucked me up," I replied. "But you, on the other hand... Mate, that is one fine piece of dick right there!"

"Awww, cheers!" he said with a smile.

We had both been slowly stroking the precursor strokes. Now it was time to get down to business.

We each fixated on the other and I admit it was very easy to get heated up with the likes of Thom

Bleaker jacking along in tandem with me. His balls did the happy dance on each upstroke, and his glistening head was a sight to behold. Seeing his foreskin pull up and down, over and up, to and fro, gave me an additional shot of sexual intensity. His dick was just so damned perfect!

He seemed to love what I was doing, too. I made sure to give him somewhat of a show, moaning and dropping the odd dirty word or phrase now and again.

My cock was really engorged, as this had been the first sexual activity I'd had since Sander and I separated.

My balls kept in tight rhythm with my strokes, and then all of a sudden I got the idea to swing around and sit up against the wall, facing Thom. This gave him not only a great view of me jacking off, but with my legs up and open, he had a clear shot at my ass and hole. I made sure to lean in such a way that the hole would naturally show.

It worked.

He started breathing even harder and was completely fixated on my ass, balls, hole, cock—especially the head—and I thought he was about to round the final turn and enter the home stretch.

I pounded my cock furiously, moving my legs, my ass, moaning in extreme pleasure, and doing all I could to make him feel good as we enjoyed each other as good friends do.

"Johnnie...." he whispered in broken breaths.

"Yeah, Thom!" I managed to reply through the intensity of our shared experience. It was feeling so wonderful. I was so looking forward to the moment that my cum would release all over me, and whatever else happened to be in the way.

"Can I cum on you? Please?"

"Sure. Where?"

"Can I cum on your balls, your cock, can I?" he moaned. I quickly nodded and he got on his knees, his massive dick just centimeters from underneath my balls and my asshole.

He leaned against the wall with his left hand, that strong hand just to the right of my face. He was breathing so hard, and I saw his right hand furiously bringing him to climax. He let out a manly groan and I felt the warmth of his cum splashing against my balls and inside my thighs.

The next huge spurts landed in my ass crack right near the hole. It felt amazing. The heat, and the feeling of it running right down my crack onto the sheet was intoxicating. Then I smelled that most wonderful of all male scents: the distinct aroma of manly cum. The seed of life. The liquid payoff that all gay men work to receive.

"Oh, God, mate! That's fucking amazing!" Thom whispered. "Are you close?"

I nodded and did nothing that would interrupt the rhythm of my hot cock. That bad boy was about to erupt, and there was at least a couple week's worth ready to explode.

"Will you cum in my mouth, Johnnie?" Thom pleaded. "I wanna taste you, mate. Please?"

I managed another nod and indicated that if he was going to get any, he'd better get in position.

He opened his mouth wide and hovered over the head of my dick, and within seconds I shot my load directly into his waiting mouth. He took in every drop and then when he knew I was done, he passionately swallowed my seed.

It took us a good fifteen minutes to recover from that very pleasant session. Two mates, respecting boundaries, and having one fucking awesome time doing what boys naturally do. Thank you, Thom. You reentered my life when I needed you the most. You are my friend, and I love you.

"HI, JOHNNIE, IT'S CRACKER JACK," the sweet voice of Jannik Hansen said when I answered my phone.

"Hey, Mister! How's tricks? I miss you!" I said. He laughed a little nervously, which could mean only one thing. "What do you want?" I joked. "You're up to no good, I can tell!"

He switched to English: "I has a porposishun and you shall hear, okay Johnnie Bond?"

"Why the English, my young Viking?" I asked him.

"For because it shall be I say this on English so noisy peoples cannot be on to my great plans!" Jannik explained.

"Who can hear you?" I asked him.

"Many spies who wanting to know my secrets!"

"Like . . ."

"Ingrid is here now. She is noisy."

"The word you're looking for is nosy. And she speaks better English than you," I said.

"Mama is here."

"She speaks better English than *me*."

"Pop is in his chair and watch the sport on the telewishun," he tried.

"Okay. He's dumb as a post when it comes to English. But the other two will figure you out. So just tell me, blockhead. What's your big plan?" I asked.

"He's moving here today and I don't want to be here more. So I say I shall move to Copenhagen and go for the school there in next week. I can be very good because I'm good, Johnnie. Can I please come for living with you there? Now?" he pleaded.

"Put Mama on the phone."

"Johnnie, please?"

"Mama. Now. Phone."

He called Magda over and handed her the phone. I could hear he was upset the way the kitchen chair scraped on the floor when he plopped down on it. I also knew he'd dropped his head into his crossed arms, onto the table. It's what he does when he thinks things aren't going his way.

"Hi, Johnnie," Mama said. "Is Copenhagen still where it's supposed to be?"

"Yep. Still here. Just like me."

"I'm very sad about what happened. I guess I should have spanked him more," she chuckled. "I think this is very bad, and I wish I had the answer."

"I do too, Mama. So I assume you heard the Spiderman's big plan?" I said.

"I did. I don't think he makes such a good secret agent," she laughed. "I'll talk to him."

"Thing is, it might be a good idea for awhile. I can only guess how things are at the house right now, and with Sander moving in it's just gonna get worse before it gets better. I wouldn't mind him being here at all," I told her.

"Both of you living on the boat? That's pretty tight living, isn't it?" she said.

"I decided I'm going house hunting starting Monday, and we'll only be on the boat until I get the new place. So talk with Niels and if it's okay with the both of you, I'll take Little Orphan Jannik in," I laughed.

She said she would, and have Jannik give me a call later. But I already knew the answer. In fact, it would give Niels and Magda time alone with the troubled one of the two sons. So I went to the grocery store and loaded up on Jannik Feed and readied his cabin for his new home.

"I CAN'T BELIEVE WE'RE HERE ON THE BOAT together," Jannik beamed. Niels had driven him in from Odense and helped him load his Legos and clothes (In that order of importance) onto the boat while I ducked out to get us a big pizza to share.

"I'm glad you're here, Cracker Jack," I told him. And it was true. I was even comforted by his presence. He was a direct link to what my life really was about. I knew I would forever be considered family by the Hansen's, and living with Jannik would be good for my psyche, I believed. Though I had to admit his resemblance to his brother was frightening. Especially from behind. But I could deal with that in time.

It had been a week since Thom rejoined his ship and sailed off below the horizon (very below as he served aboard a submarine!), and I thought of him often. But not as often as I did Sander, despite the surprise dick pic he'd left for me on my phone. Cheeky bugger!

Jannik wove himself into my daily fabric as if things had always been this way. He was a delight in every way, insisting on doing all the chores aboard, and preparing his school audition piece while being considerate to the neighbors and my sleep schedule. There was no denying that Niels and Magda had raised their children properly. Sander included.

And as angry as Jannik was towards his brother, he never decimated him verbally or spoke unfairly

313

against him. He just didn't say anything about him, which today is quite a notable feat among people.

Jannik also displayed maturity in his daily routine. He got himself up in the morning, showered once or twice a day, did his (and my) laundry without prompting, washed up the galley after we ate, and got himself to bed at a reasonable hour. Again, I credit my in-laws for that. I know for a fact that I was never that way, and I consider myself a pretty good guy.

Marge came by for a visit and Jannik was all glee and joy when he saw her coming down the gangway. We played Risk (Marge kicked ass), chess (neither stood a chance against me—it was a slaughter), and Monopoly (Marge and I wound up homeless against Jannik Trump).

She stayed the night with us and took us all to breakfast in the morning. What a wonderful time that was.

Marge and Jannik took a walk along the pier and she asked him what he knew about Sander. She didn't get much out of him with the exception of a G-rated version of his opinion of his brother. She never once brought Sander up to me, for which I was grateful.

The next week brought school for my young shipmate. By the end of the second week everybody knew him and he had at least a dozen close friends. No surprise there. He just told everyone he knew that he was living with his brother on his boat (well, I'm still his brother-in-law, so it's kind of true), and that we were looking for a house.

That week we found one, and I put an offer in which was accepted. We'd get the keys the following week.

Things were going great. I was adjusting to my loss, was starting a new life, and had even received a couple of letters from Thom. I was still very sad, of course, but things were steadily, if slowly, moving in the right direction. So of course a major problem had to slam me full bore, right in the face. And I never saw this one coming.

Chapter 23

OH, BROTHER

J ANNIK'S BEST NEW MATE AT HIS NEW

school is a boy called Florian. A very nice kid, if a bit on the exuberant side, he and Jan get along like nobody's business. So it was no problem when he asked if he could visit his friend over the weekend at his home in nearby Herlev. Of course he could. So I drove him over, met Florian's mom, and left them to enjoy their weekend together.

When I returned to the boat I thought it'd be a treat to lie down and stretch out on the big bed in my cabin and take a nap. No clock watching. No worries. Just sleep for awhile.

There was a five page letter waiting on my pillow.

My dear wonderful awesome beautiful excellent fantastic Johnnie.

I have make you this letter and have go through and cheque every word to make sure it is spell right because I want you to understand all I write to you today right now.

What my brother have do to you is more than very bad. It is criminal. It is so bad there not is words to say how much bad. I want you to know I hate him and things will not be the same with us forever times. I know what you will say about that, I do, Johnnie.

So please do forgive me for what I say just now but it is so very much the truth. I am not so good as you, and so you must

318

forgive how I feel about him.

Nothing I can do about this except to try and not think of what he have do.

I wish to tell you some thing, what is so very big to me and I plead that you will listen to my voice about this. Please, Johnnie.

There is a fact. There is such a fact that I can not deny this and I will not try to deny this.

You will remembers I get in much troubles in the pass because I see you and him having love together. You know I have watch you both in the bed and this is very bad awful. But there is one thing I not have tell the doctor or you or anyone. So I say it now. And it is hundred percent positive and true. Like you and him and one at my school in Korup, I am very hundred percent gay. This I know since age of eight years Johnnie.

So I be honest with you and tell you one time for sure. And please forgive what I am to say

next, but I have to say it or I can
not feel right.

Johnnie Allen, I love you, of
course. But what you do not know is
that I am in love with you. I have
been for two years, and I never
said why to the doctor or to you
why I watch you and him that times
in your room. It because I was
watching YOU, Johnnie. It because
I true do love you. It not a stupid
pup love, or infatuation. It not is
because I am near 14 and so have a
child's feelings. It is because I
love you. Everything about you.

You make all good for
everybody, always. You think of
others before yourself and I have
try to do this myself too just
because of you. And you are so
handsome and sporty look. I am not
a silly boy. I am not gay because I
want to be like you. I am gay
because that is how I am made. And
you are the dream of my whole life.

Yes I have had one kind of
like a boyfriend in my whole life.
That one is my best friend, Preben.

I care deep for him, and have only be with him. But this is only because I know I can never ever be with you. That you are marry to my brother. But now thing have change. They have change in a very big way and so I ask you now.

Johnnie, is it possible that you could ever love me like you did for my brother? I know we have an age issue for now, but in one and one half short years it not be a problem at all. This you know. If you even think there is possible of this, may I make you some promise?

First, I swear to all in my life, on my life, on Mama's life, and on your life that I will NEVER ever do to you what my brother have do. NEVER. I love you so very much that you can not even understand how it is possible.

I know it will be awkward at the start, but we can live or move anywhere that you want or need to go. Even United States if you want after I am 18 years. Perhaps U.K. We have friends there, and you one

time said you could move there
with your job if you like.

I promise I will do nothing
but love and support you, just as
you have done so for me, and all
who we know, and my idiot brother.

I know I take a risk to even
show these feelings to you because
what if something happen and you
and he gets back together. Then I
will has show my poker hand. But
you know what? I don't care because
the possible that I could be with
you as your man for the whole rest
of my life is more important then
if I get embarrass. So I tell you
this truthful.

Now let say you are open to
this idea. I promise that I will not
insist for sex with you until I am
15 years so you don't feel like the
law is be break, or that those
think that what we do are wrong.

As far as all concern, you are
just my relative who let me lives
with you for school in Copenhagen.
And I will promise I not will have
sex with NOBODY EVER until it can

be with you. That I swear to you. I will still jack off like a zoo monkey three time a day (and be think of you when I do it) but I promise I only do it when you not are there or can't see and perhaps be embarrass. I also swear I shall not try and get looks of you naked or anything of sex to keep things like they shall be until I am 15 years.

You also know I do not think like a child, Johnnie. You know I am always have be comfortable with adults not peoples my own age. This have always be the case. I can relate with you as an adult. I will never be a bothersome troublesome child. You won't has to take care from me. We takes care of each others on an adult level. Does that seem good for you? Also, you know I have many skill that most adult do not have that we can use together. I can build, work all tools, and I know things that can be of help to us.

Long Before Morning

So I guess here is the part when I say it is all up for you now.

I have open my heart 100% and I have hold not one thing behind. So if you love me in this way, or think you can someday love me in this way, will you please let me know? I love you so much, Johnnie. I always will even if you decide another way. But please think of this very serious. Because I means every single word of it.

I love you. Much love from Jannik Hansen.

OH FOR FUCK'S SAKE! Of all the times for this to happen. Of course I already know the answer, but how do I tell Jannik that? It'll break his sweet little heart! *Goddamn fucking shit Christ on a sidecar!* Is there no end to this carnival known as my life?!

What the hell do I do first? Call his mom? Talk with Pop? Talk to him? His doctor? *Shit!* First Thom appears out of nowhere. Literally! And now I find out that the sweetest little kid *who's the same age as my own sister and brother back in the States* has been crushing on me for two years? And he's gay?! What is it with these Hansen boys, that they always appear to be straight as arrows but then turn out to be bent as nails?! God, guys, put on some lipstick or swish a little or something! You're blindsiding me here!

Okay, okay, think, Allen! How do you handle this? And don't fucking google it, either! You're on your own here. Deal with it!

SANDER WAS BESIDE HIMSELF with grief. It was like he was mourning a death. The problem was, he was the killer. And the fact he freely admitted this failed to make it any easier.

He decided this day to commit what amounted to emotional suicide by visiting all of the places that held wonderful memories of their time together. He began after breakfast by glancing through Mama's photo album. There they were, happy as could be. The body language in all of the photographs oozed nothing but pure love and joy.

Long Before Morning

There were the shots of the house in Gelsted. Jannik's wolf pups. Their trip to Tampa to see Springsteen in concert. The time they went to London to see *Chess—The Concert* was captured for all eternity. He remembered that night. Oh, there's Jannik standing outside the World Court in The Netherlands—they all shared a pile of pot brownies back in the hotel later that night and, like the brownies, got incredibly baked.

And then he turned the page and saw their wedding.

Sander gently closed the hefty album and headed for his car. He drove to Gelsted and walked the grounds a little. There was the little knoll where he had dispersed the cremated remains of his former lover, Torben. It seemed like forever ago. Johnnie had been so kind to allow the man to stay with them while he fought the good fight in his last days of AIDS. Johnnie loved me so much, he thought, that I could bring my high school boyfriend who had hurt me so much here to live with us. Without resentment. Without conditions.

That's when Sander cried. He would sob buckets quite often that day, and he now understood firsthand what the Scrooge character must have felt in Dickens' *A Christmas Carol* when he was whisked off to the different places by the ghosts. Scrooge discovered that he was riddled with regret.

So, too, was Sander Lars Hansen. But unlike old Scrooge who was given the opportunity to make everything right that fine Christmas morning, Sander knew that he wouldn't enjoy such an outcome. *Johnnie wasn't a fool,* he thought. *So why would he ever give a shit like me another chance after what I'd done?*

The rest of the day was spent contemplating what was next. He had to meet Johnnie in the lawyer's office on Thursday, on the next day the paperwork would be forwarded to the judge and finalized. He would be alone and forever not a part of Johnnie's life. *Why did I do it? Idiot!!!*

Sander drove into town and past the train station where he had delivered and collected Johnnie so many times. It was also where he followed him onto the platform to ask if he could ride the train with him into Copenhagen. That day became the night they first made love after mutually confessing their affection for one another. Johnnie was everywhere. That's because Johnnie was his world, and Sander had spun that world off its axis. Where it would land probably wouldn't bode well for him.

After having a dinner plate at their favorite downtown pub, he skulked home. He was glad to end this day even though another one just like it was on its tail. He started the car after a long sigh and pulled onto Østre stationsvej, to Rugårdsvej, and home to his parents.

Chapter 24

CRESCENDO

EVERYTHING I HAD REHEARSED IN MY

head while Jannik was at Florian's evaporated the moment I saw him trotting down the dock. Mid-morning on this gorgeous Sunday would be my grownup showdown with my favorite lad. I would do anything to avoid hurting his feelings, but this had to be settled now.

Jannik smiled when he saw me and called, "Permission to come aboard, Skipper Johnnie!"

"Aye, matey! Haul your anchor over here!" I responded. He hopped aboard and tossed his backpack into the cabin. "You guys have a good time?" I asked him, as we ducked into the saloon.

"The best! Florian's dad has a big train set and some really great old records. It's in their basement. And we had lots of Cokes and hot dogs and we made nachos, and Florian's dad said that electric trains are the original video game!"

"Lots of tracks and switch points, and stations and things?" I asked him. He said not only that, but there was a whole town and he even made a model of Amalienborg Palace right smack in the middle of the layout.

"I'm glad Florian's my friend," Jannik said. "Sometime you should go and see the trains."

"That sounds awesome, Cracker Jack," I said. Then it was time. "So I have an idea..."

"Great! You always have the best ones!"

"We have some business to do, you and me, and then afterwards I think we should go for dinner at the Modern American Diner," I said. "I know how much you like it, so what do you say?"

Jannik smiled and quickly nodded. He knew where this was going, so he settled in and waited for me to begin.

I presented the letter and said, "I read this very well-written, and very beautiful letter from one of my favorite people in the whole wide world," I began. "In fact, it was so lovely and wonderful do ya know what I did?"

Jannik shook his head and softly said no. I continued, "I cried. I was so happy that you wrote such powerful and honest words to me, Jan, and because I write too, I could appreciate them so much."

"So what will we do?" he asked. "I mean every word in there, you know?"

"I do know. I can see that. But there are so many things to consider, and we're both so clever and smart that I know we'll make the right decision, don't you think?" I said. Jannik nodded slowly.

"I'm not normal," he declared. "Everybody knows it. I'm not like regular kids, if that's what you mean."

"I prefer to think you're exceptional," I told him. "Because what exactly is normal, anyway? But the problem as I see it is that even if you're wiser, more mature, and above your grade in the way you think... You know there's no way that we could be together in the way you suggested. It's just not right, Jannik."

"Do you love me?"

"That has nothing to do with it. And I know that *you* know that," I replied.

"Do you love me?!" he forcefully asked.

"Jan, I love you in so many ways. I love your

331

heart, your humongous brain, your sweet nature. But the very real fact is that I'm twenty-four years old, and you won't be fourteen until April. I was eleven years old when Mama had you," I reminded him. "So even if I was madly in love with you, there's absolutely no way we could be together. Don't you understand that, Jan?"

"But I told you I would wait! I said I wouldn't push you in any way. When I'm fifteen we're totally legal in Denmark, so what's the problem? We can make this work, Johnnie. I promise we can," he pleaded.

"That's right. And when you're fifteen I'll be twenty-six. And every year it'll be the same. There's just too much here, and besides, I'm not even away from Sander yet. Jannik, sweet man, I have to say no. I really, really do. And I love you! I always have, and I always will," I honestly told him.

"You won't change your mind?" he asked.

"Absolutely no way, Jan. And you know I'm making the best decision for both of us. I promise you that. And truth told, I know that you know that," I said. And believe it or not, he took it well.

"Can I still stay with you?" he asked.

"Of course you can. I love it that you're here," I told him. "I feel so damned lucky, and I feel sorry for

Mama and Pop because I'm the one that gets to keep you for a while," I exclaimed. "You are a joy to be around, and whatever boy ends up taking you home with him will be the luckiest boy in the world, I swear."

"Your ex used to be the luckiest boy in the world, but not anymore," Jannik said.

"Well, sometimes things change and there's nothing anyone can do about it. So you just learn to deal with it however it comes, I guess," I said.

"How do you keep from just smashing his face in, Johnnie?" Jannik asked me.

"Because I love him more than my own life, that's how."

Jannik asked, "How can you? And if you do love him that much, why don't you guys just get back together then?"

"I love your brother absolutely not one whole millimeter less than before. But to answer your question, Jan, it's that no matter what, I can't trust him. And that's what nobody seems to understand. I can't ever trust Sander again, and if I can't trust him, I just can't be with him," I explained.

"Okay," Jannik said, "I understand. And thanks."

"What for?" I asked him.

"For treating me with dignity. I mean, I don't

know anyone else who would have been like you are with me right now. So, thanks," Jannik said.

"Well... You're welcome, I guess."

"And I'm sorry if my letter embarrassed you, or made you think I'm a nut case or something. You can just tear it up, okay?"

I looked him in the eye and reached over to hug him. "Jannik Hansen, you'll have to take this letter away from me with a Glock 19 and a slew of hollow point bullets. And even then I won't give it up," I told him. "This letter is one of the most precious things I'll ever own."

"Whatever," he replied. "Do we got any orange juice? I'm sick of Cokes."

I HAVEN'T SMILED ONCE SINCE Johnnie left. Now my brother hates me, and he's even moved in with him on the boat. And I heard Mama tell Pop that he bought a house.

Johnnie said I could keep our home in Gelsted, and that he'd even pay off the bank. It would be mine, but I'm not going to take it. I just don't deserve a thing, so I'm not going to take a thing.

When we're at the lawyer's on Thursday, I'll make sure he takes back the annuity he made for me, too. Everything's gone to shit, and I'm the one that shoveled it. Huh. What I did was worse than what Torben did to me. Imagine that.

I have to see the doctor. I'll call and make an appointment tomorrow because I have got to find out what's wrong with me once and for all. I can't live like this anymore.

JANNIK AND I DECIDED TO WALK from the marina over to the Modern American Diner. I have to say, being a diner and drive-in aficionado from way back—thank you, Grampy!—these guys do a great job.

The atmosphere is perfect, and the food tastes like my favorite greasy spoon back home. Jannik loves the idea that he's eating the kinds of things I grew up on, and it doesn't matter what time of day it is, he always goes for the biscuits and country gravy.

We scooted into the red sparkly booth with the stainless steel trim and each grabbed a menu. Jannik glanced at his and tossed it on the table.

"Guess!" he dared me.

"B and G!" I answered.

"Give that man a cigar!" he smiled. "And can I get some French fries, too?" Of course, I said. I decided on the classic double cheeseburger and fries, with a slice of cherry pie.

"So Jan, something we haven't talked about yet," I said. "In your letter you made something very clear."

"You mean that I like guys?" he answered. "Well, I do. It's a fact."

"You're a hundred percent sure?"

"Yep. I am. Not interested in girls that way in one little bit. Not even half a bit," he said. "But I know I like boys. Boys turn me on; girls do not."

"Okay, then. So have you had any physical experiences yet? And pounding your pud doesn't count." Jan nodded, not fazed at all by the directness of the question.

"Yeah. Preben. We've done it a lot."

"Is he gay too, then?" I asked him.

Jannik thought for a moment and said, "Well, he won't say. He talks about girls, but then he loves that he wears fingernail polish and he totally likes all of the fag-hag singers..."

"Fag-hag singers?"

"Yeah. Katy Perry, Adele, Bette Midler, Alison Moyet, Barbra Streisand, you know. Girls who appeal to fags like Preben!" he laughed.

"Ahhh... I see."

We turned our orders in to our waitress and talked about school and all of the exciting things he was looking forward to, and then our great day turned black. I swear, that fucking raincloud that keeps following me around is gonna get it one of these days!

The Modern American Diner does attract a local crowd, but its main clientele happens to be fish-out-of-water American tourists who fear the local cuisine. So there's always a brash, loud group of crass citizens of my homeland ready to embarrass America abroad. And they always seem to wind up at the diner.

The whole time we were there we were forced to listen to this obnoxious asshole as he continued to chastise his wife and children, and he didn't care who heard him.

He bitched out his wife for transgressions known only to him. His four children appeared terrified of his every move. They would flinch, and the tone of his voice was so demeaning. His little girl continually kept her head down, and his two sons were blank as robots. One would think by the way he verbally attacked them that they were the ones responsible for all of the ills of the world.

Then, when their food finally arrived at the table, he piously led his little sheep in a word of prayer. Okay, major flashbacks of the PTSD variety were washing over me right about then.

Jannik was watching with disgust as well, and he dropped a comment or two that more than illustrated the point. What happened next, from the tipping of the milk glass, is unknown to me. Jannik told me everything that happened later.

The older son, a thinly built kid around eleven or twelve years old, reached for a bottle of ketchup. In doing so, his elbow knocked over his younger brother's glass of milk. The dad exploded. He called the boy some awful names and then picked up his fork, turned it so the four sharp tines were aimed at his son, and then with a flick of his wrist he slapped the boy in his forehead with the fork.

Four tiny holes in the boy's skin produced four trickles of blood, and the kid began to cry.

The next thing I remember is that I was in the back seat of a taxi crying my eyes out, Jannik in the front passenger seat looking right at me, telling me it was all okay.

Here's what happened.

Apparently I completely lost my shit. I saw the blood and the kid's tears and according to Jan I jumped out of our booth and in two strides was behind the dad.

I had grabbed him around his neck and literally pulled him up and over his chair, and then I was told that I threw him against a wall with a picture of James Dean and slugged him square in the face—1-2-3-4 times. Hard.

Jan said that nobody in the diner even acted as if they were going to try and stop me, and that some of them were egging it on.

The kids and the wife just sat and watched it. None of them seemed to be upset about it at all.

After I had slugged him in the face, Jan said I swung him around and he fell to the floor at that point. He said I was yelling things at the man, but they sounded inhuman—like some kind of satanic voice or something. Like a demon in a horror movie. He said there were words, but he couldn't understand them.

The last thing I did, according to Jan, was that I took a stainless steel water pitcher from a serving stand and clocked him in the head with it about half a dozen times. That's when the cab driver, who was having his break, grabbed Jan and they helped me to my feet and hustled me out of the door and into his taxi. I woke up, or came to, or whatever you want to call it right there in his cab.

Jan said the staff and the manager of the diner never even considered calling the police, and in fact the manager had held the door open so they could get me safely into the taxi and away.

We got back to the boat and I asked Jan if he would get my wallet out so we could pay the driver, but he absolutely would not take our money. He said that everyone in the place applauded what I had done, and that if I hadn't beaten everyone to it, somebody else would have done the same or worse to the fucker. So that was our nice dinner out, thank you very much.

It took quite awhile to return to normal after that, but I knew things were getting okay again when Jannik came into my room around ten o'clock and said, "Hey, Incredible Hulk, mind if I order us a pizza to be delivered?"

The start of another uneventful week in the life of Johnnie Fucking Allen. "Yeah, Mike Tyson, go ahead and order a pizza. Make it big."

I love that kid!

Chapter 25

THE TIME HAD COME. THIS WAS THE

day that my life would change forever. Pen would be put to paper and the marriage between Johnnie Paul Allen of Auburn, Washington, USA, citizen of the United States of America, to Sander Lars Hansen, natural born citizen of Odense, in the Kingdom of Denmark, would be unceremoniously dissolved. Ended. Curtain dropped.

When I arrived at the lawyer's, Sander—nicely dressed and unfairly wearing his Blue Stratos body spray—was already waiting there with Mama. She suggested she go with him because she didn't think he'd be in any condition to drive afterwards.

Nice one, Mama! I gotta hand it to ya: mother guilt and manipulation skillfully well played right there!

"Good, Mama. That's good," I said, offering her a hug. "Nice to see you guys. Hi, Sander."

"Hi, Johnnie," Sander replied. "You look really nice."

"Well so do you," I said. "You always do," I told him. And I meant it. The lawyer and his clerk entered the office and invited us to sit down. He didn't waste a second.

"Mister Allen, you are the filer, and Mister Hansen, you are the recipient, yes?" he asked. We both agreed and he handed me a rather expensive pen. "Mister Allen, if you'll just sign here, I'll serve your partner with the writ of divorce and once he signs, we'll file with the court."

He informed Sander that he was being sued for a non-contested divorce, and was invited to sign the paper. As he bent over the desk to affix his signature, I noticed tears rolling down his cheeks. Without pause the lawyer's clerk offered him some tissues. Mama stood behind Sander with her loving hand on her son's back, knowing as I did the pain her boy was experiencing in that moment.

Sander laid the pen on the desk and sat down on the chair, burying his face in his hands, his shoulders trembling. I caught Mama's eye and she indicated that it would be okay if I went ahead and left them there. But I just stood there.

I walked over to him and placed my hand on his shoulder. He never looked up, but he rested his hand on mine and gave it the longest squeeze. I felt the regret and the apology he was delivering in that grip, and when he drew his hand back I patted and stroked his hair one last time, bent down and kissed the top of his head, told him that I loved him and that I always would, and left the room as shattered as he was.

I don't remember the drive home, which is proof that I shouldn't have been driving. Once again, Mama was right. Sander likely would have wound up in a ditch driving himself all the way back to Odense, and the only reason that I didn't myself was because there aren't any ditches in central Copenhagen.

When I got back to the boat I headed straight for my bed and unleashed the cry of the century. It was four hours of tears, moans, sniffles, itchy eyes, and flashes of memories that would never be recreated again. I saw his face. I smelled his scent. I could feel him all around me. This is what death was like.

It was too early to call anyone back in the States, and the only one I could've called anyway was Grampy, and he didn't need to hear me blubbering on the phone from five thousand miles away.

Based on the shadows crossing the cabin the sun was getting lower. I got up to use the bathroom and figured I might as well stay up. Hell, I didn't know what I was figuring. I felt lost.

"Johnnie?" It was Jannik on the other side of the door. "Can I come in?"

"Sure, Cracker Jack. I'm decent," I told him. He cautiously pushed open the door, peeking his head around, and of course in the fading light he was the exact duplicate of his brother. "How you doing?" I asked him.

"I brought this for you," he said, handing me a bottle of spring water. "You're probably gonna dry out soon if you don't put some of this back inside of you."

"Thanks, buddy. That's sweet of you." I drank down the whole bottle and sat up on the bed. Jannik came in and joined me.

Jannik asked me, "Are you gonna be okay? Should I call Mama and Pop to come help you?"

"Nah, I'll be okay. That was a couple of weeks worth of crying that I'd saved up. After today I thought I'd get rid of it," I told him. "How long have you been out there?

"Since four. I had to make sure you were okay."

"You're a good guy, did you know that?" I asked him. He shot me a little smile and leaned his head against my arm.

"So are you, Johnnie."

———————

ANOTHER WEEK WENT BY. Marge came and stayed with me one night just to see how I was getting on. She asked me when I felt I'd be ready to return to the land of the living and come back to work. I told her she could schedule me anytime.

She checked out the house I'd bought. She loved it, and we enthusiastically discussed decorating ideas. Jannik measured out the footprint of his new studio he was planning upstairs, and excitedly reported that he'd even have room for a vocal booth.

Long Before Morning

The next day we slowly started making the move from *Stargazer* to the new house, and Jannik and I went to the paint store to get the supplies to redo the walls. I also hired a flooring guy to come in and build up the poly coats on the wooden floors. Nothing like moving into a new place to keep your mind off of things. Except I didn't.

Then came the day.

An email from a friend of mine in the States dropped into my mailbox. Sander had written him asking if he would forward a note from him to me because he didn't think I would open an email directly from him. I would have, but I thanked the friend and took my laptop into my cabin and sat at my little writing desk. I opened the attachment.

Dear Johnnie

Of course you know who it is. I want to try one more last and final time to see if maybe we can be together again.

    I am so very sorry for what I did for you. For what I did to us. I destroyed our family. We are a family, a perfect family you and me, and I destroyed it. I can never take it back. I was and am stupid, but I know who you are. I do.

I know your heart. I know it so well that it breaks my heart to think of what I did to us.

I hurt your feelings in the worst way. I do not deserve you, <u>and I know now that's why I did what I did.</u>

I can say it was because of Per Larsen and some schoolboy fantasy I had for him, but it would be a lie. And the last thing you need is for me to lie to you. I was mistaken. I was so stupid, and I'm glad that everyone knows how much of an asshole I am. I deserve it.

I probably have not lost just you, either. I know that Jannik hates me. I wish Palle and Ingrid have not pull him off of me at the house, because I deserve for him to beat me up a lot worse. I ruined his life, too.

I know you have forgiven me. I know that you have do this, Johnnie, because I feel that you have.

I know that you have no reason to ever trust me again. I do not deserve a second chance. I definitely do not deserve anything. But can we talk? <u>Can I let you know exactly what I think I can do to make this work again?</u>

If you give me the opportunity to speak with you, I promise you this: You will never have to worry about something like this ever happens again. I promise I will work with your doctor about how you feel that I deserve all this beautiful life that you gave me.

I will repair the wall around my family. And I'm willing to take as much time as you need before you even half trust me again.

Johnnie, I can not imagine a life that is good without you in it. I promise that I will always be what we once had, if you just want to try again.

I have read the two books you have write about us just so I can feel us together again. And now I'm almost done with the second and I do not want to see it ends there. There must be more after that.

I was a stupid kid. Let me prove to you that I am worth to be your husband again. I miss you. I miss our life so much.

I miss waking up with your beautiful body beside me. I miss your beautiful yellow hair, your touch, your smell. I miss your heart and humor. Be so kind Johnnie – Please.

You do not have to marry me again. We can just start again as lovers again until you feel safe with me. Johnnie, not only have I not, or even want to have sex with anyone. I have not even masturbate in all the time we have be apart. Not means anything without you, and I pray that we try again.

If we do that, I promise that you will never have to worry about anything like what I did for you ever happening again. I love you. With all my love and heart,

Sander Lars Hansen but you may call me Pokey if you like.

So the little fucker sure can write. I'll give him that. I didn't know what to think. I love him. That's not in question; never was.

I need him. I always will, no matter what life brings in the future. No matter how good it becomes, there will always be a gigantic hole that can only be filled by him.

God! For fuck's sake!

I'm going to bed.

Chapter 26

THREE IN THE MORNING. THERE'S

no way I was going to get anymore sleep this night. Sander Lars Hansen. Sander Lars Hansen. Sander . . .

"Come on, Jan, get up," I said, shaking the little guy's shoulder. "Get dressed. We're going to Mama and Pop's place."

"What the...?"

"Come on, sailor. Hit the deck. Grab your jacket and some Legos and let's blow this pop stand!"

Within ten minutes we were on the E-20 bound for Odense.

"What are we doing?" Jannik asked with a deep yawn. "Why are we going home?"

"Fuck if I know," I admitted. And I didn't know, although I did. A little over an hour and we were there.

The familiar and homey smells of the loving home greeted us, and Jannik just zombie walked to his bedroom and crashed. He didn't even take his clothes off. He was out.

I took in the main room, the nucleus of every family in the world. I'd spent so many happy times in this room. There were pictures on the walls, Mama's proof that she had raised an incredible family and had done it well. There I was in a family grouping. There was Sander and me standing together on the patio holding spatulas, both wearing chef aprons. His said *He's American* with an arrow pointed in my direction. Mine said, *I can't help it.*

There was one of me and Pop in our tighty whities acting like we were weight lifters. Ingrid was the weight bar that we held over our smiling faces.

I walked up the stairs and on the wall to my

left the complete photographic history of the three Hansen kids was displayed in calendar order.

Sander sitting with Pop not a day over five; tiny Jannik sitting on the potty; Ingrid in her ballet clothes—she despised ballet. There's Sander on the riser at the zoo so he could pet the elephant.

And at the top of the stairs, a picture of Sander's fifteenth birthday cake. He's blowing out the candles, and in exactly six months from the time Ingrid snapped that picture he would walk into my life.

And now I was standing outside his door. The words he had written to me hadn't stopped replaying since I read them. They were honest and true, of that I had no doubt. He was desperate to save what we had, and he was prepared to do everything he could to do it—but to do it within the confines of honesty.

He had poured his heart out, true enough, and he had hit all the right notes. But then he wrote something that I could not ignore.

Many people before us have been in this position. And many will again. A relationship—a healthy one, anyway—relies on two things: honesty and deference. You have to defer to the other one's needs, and if both of you do this and you are at all times honest with the one you love, that is what actually makes the love that you have for one another sustainable. We had that. And I thought it was lost for good.

I do not deserve you, <u>and I know now that's why I did what I did.</u>

It wasn't about me. It was because he didn't feel that he was good enough for me. Well, Mister Hansen, I'm here, right now, sitting on the floor of your childhood bedroom to let you know, sir, that you are completely full of shit.

And furthermore, young man, we are going to get to the bottom of this if it kills us.

You are the fucking light of my life. It's me who doesn't deserve you. I dreamed about you my whole life.

You were with me when that fucking piece

of shit step "dad" was beating my ass for being who I was and am.

You were Zac Hanson when I dreamed of having a playmate I could unabashedly love.

You were with me aboard the cargo ship when I looked to the horizon wondering who and where the hell you are.

When I was streaming across the sky over your God blessed country, looking down over the gentle green rolling landscape that is your kingdom, and wondering about my friends and life that awaited me below the belly of that airliner, it was *you* who held the welcome sign.

I was born to be here with you, and I believe it's the same for you. So enough of this bullshit. Enough of pride, ego, and my stupid hurt feelings. I am your man, like it or not, Sander Lars Hansen, and I thank the stars that you chose not to give up on us.

I forgave you the instant I was wronged. Why? Because I love you. Was I shattered? Yes, in that moment. Why? *Because I love you.*

How, dear sweet man, can you think for an instant that I'm somehow not good enough for you? You are perfection to me. You are the key to my existence and I freely give it to you.

> I know you have forgiven me. I know that you have do this, Johnnie, because I feel that you have.
> I know that you have no reason to ever trust me again. I do not deserve a second chance. I definitely do not deserve anything. But can we talk? <u>Can I let you know exactly what I think I can do to make this work again?</u>

You've already let me know, Sander. And I'm here. So right now I will lean against the wall with the rocket ship wallpaper, take your hand in mine, watch you sleep, and be here when you wake up in the morning. I won't take my eyes off of you, and if you'll have me, I'll never be apart from you ever again. In this life, or the next one after that.

IT WAS A LITTLE AFTER SEVEN when Sander Lars

Hansen woke up. He was shocked, to say the least. All I could do was smile at him when he rolled on the bed and pushed onto his knees. Then the room went still for a good five seconds.

"Good morning, Pokey."

"It's you! And you called me Pokey! And I love you so much!" Sander cried with joy. He unabashedly crawled and jumped from the bed right into my arms, and then we cried together for a good half hour. No words were exchanged. We were just there, together, as we should be.

"Is this for real, Johnnie Allen?" he smiled through tears of joy. All I could do was nod. He hugged me tighter, and I just reveled in the feeling of having him in my arms once more. This time nothing would ever come between us. I was sure of it.

After we dried out a little, we went downstairs to the kitchen holding hands, standing together in the entryway. Mama and Pop were in the midst of their breakfast, and Pop's face was hidden by the *Fyens Stiftstidende* newspaper. He lowered the newspaper enough to see us and quipped, "Mama, it looks like the paper went with the wrong headline this morning."

She was already on her feet, and fully bawling by the time she reached us with her open arms.

We just stood there for a minute while it all sunk in. "Is it true?" she cried.

"Yes, Mama. It's forever true," Sander replied. I don't think I'd ever seen that big of a grin on his face. And my heart was bursting with joy.

"I have to call your sister! Sit down and eat, you two. You've both lost too much weight over this. Sit!" she ordered. Pop chuckled and said maybe he should break up with Mama for a few weeks so he could lose a few kilos himself.

Listening to Mama on the phone was so funny. She was like an old Jewish mother who was happy that her kids had finally gotten their shit together. But the funniest exchange?

Mama: "But your brother and Johnnie are back together, Ingrid! Tell Palle he can do that to you anytime!

Ingrid: Mama! Stop!

Mama: Besides, it's too early in the day for that horseplay. Wait till the sun goes down! Now get over here!

Jannik stumbled in half asleep, haven been awakened by all of the commotion downstairs.

"I knew it. You caved in, didn't you?" he asked me.

"It's called love, Jannik, and someday you'll have someone and you'll know what it means. Stop being a brat and be happy for us," I told him.

"So are you happy then? The both of you?"

"Yes," I said. "Very."

"More than you'll ever know, Spiderman," Sander added.

Jannik plopped down in his chair and filled a bowl with Corn Flakes. Then he looked at his brother and me and simply said, "Then I'm happy. Mama, I need to get some underwear because I forgot mine and there's none in my drawer.

"What are you wearing now, then?" Mama asked.

Jan said, matter-of-fact, "Nothing. I'm just free ballin' it.

Chapter 27

BLANK SLATE

MUCH HAPPENED IN THE WEEKS

following our reconciliation. Things went back to normal in some ways, and in others we found ourselves on the learning curve. And that was a healthy thing.

And we agreed on one thing very quickly. That night we would leave Jan with the folks and start having some 'us' time, beginning with a trip to Room 22 of the 71 Nyhavn hotel on the wharf in Copenhagen. That's the very place where Sander and I first discovered one another, and the official start of our romance together.

We were a little disappointed to find that the room was already taken when we called ahead that afternoon for reservations. Sander asked for the phone, and he took over while I went upstairs and packed his things.

When we checked in at the hotel I was surprised to learn that he had already paid for the room, and that he had reserved the very best suite in the place. Two bedrooms, a huge Jacuzzi in the middle of the room, even a fully stocked bar that was included in the price.

The elevator stopped on the second floor, and I just followed him. This was his show, and I felt pretty special I must say. So imagine my surprise when we stopped outside our old room. Sander knocked on the door.

We heard voices and footsteps and soon a very lovely woman answered the door.

"Hello, can I help you?" she asked. She sounded like she was from the west of Denmark. Maybe Aarhus.

"Yes, hello. I hope you can. This room is very special to my man and me. It's where we fell in love. And we'd very much like to sleep here tonight," Sander began.

"Oh, I see..." she replied. "But of course we're here and..."

"That's why I did what I did. You see, here's the key to the biggest suite in the place. There's bedrooms, a free bar, and a hot tub in the middle of the room. So if you'll agree to stay there tonight, we'll trade you," Sander explained. I was absolutely floored. What a little operator, my Sander.

"Hey, Tobias! You've got to hear this! Come here!" she said, laughing at the absurdity of it all. And of course we got the room.

We went downstairs and had a dinner of thick tournedos, one of the best cut steaks in the world, and shared a bottle of wine.

Then we loaded up on snacks and sodas at the 7-11 up the way and returned to 'our' room. The couple had left us a cute note on the bed and had gone to a lot of trouble to straighten the place up. We were sure they were enjoying the suite.

Then it was time for bed. And I do mean *bed.*

"I cannot be held responsible for what is about to happen, Johnnie Allen, so you must forgive me if I break any laws of nature or Her Majesty's government in the next three hours," Sander smiled.

"What? Only three hours? Fuck that shit! Try all damned night, Pokey!" I countered. "If we're not sore and raw by morning, I want my money back!"

He pushed me onto the bed and pulled off my shoes, jeans, and underwear. Then he yanked off my shirt over my head. He was kind enough to leave my socks on, the little rapist.

In seconds he was down to his bare bones, and speaking of bones, there his was. Extended like a flagpole over the entrance to a building, I couldn't resist. I sat up on the edge of the bed and took him into my mouth, furiously sucking his beautiful cock while I slowly stroked my own.

"I'm just warning you, Johnnie Allen, that it won't be me who cums first!" He laughed. "I'm gonna be your Viking sex machine for the foreseeable future, and time after that!"

I pulled off of his dick for enough time to tell him that I wouldn't be answering him for awhile as I had a big Viking cock in my mouth. So shut up and moan!

I sucked him for a good half hour and he suddenly dropped to his knees and took mine in his sweet mouth. The way he would roll his tongue over and around my head was just so fucking sexy. What a turn on!

Then he gently pushed me from a sitting position onto my back and opened my asshole with a couple of spitty fingers. He never changed his sucking rhythm as he explored my ass, sending true shivers up my spine.

"Oh my fuck!" I managed to say. "Oh, Sander, that's fucking awesome, dude!"

Now he was darting his fingers into and out of my hole at double the pace of his sucking. Then he put his mouth to my balls and started licking and sucking on them like a sex crazed maniac! My sex crazed maniac!

Without interruption he crawled up under my legs causing my knee joints to rest upon his shoulders. Now, with my ass lifted and in position, he went down on my with a rim job that must have lasted close to an hour. And then he rolled me over and continued licking my hole while I was positioned doggy-style.

Soon we climbed fully onto the bed and we faced each other, kissing for the longest time. He held my face in his hands and kept kissing me between exclamations of his love for me.

We were nonstop. And each couldn't get enough of the other. I was almost perplexed because I wanted to do everything with him at once. Then I took my turn.

I laid him spread eagle on the bed and dived my face into his beautiful ass. The salty, savory musk of his perfectly shaped and spotlessly clean hole rose up to meet my twitching tongue.

Sander shoved a pillow under his pelvis which put him in the perfect position to receive this loving gesture, and I didn't fail him.

Finally, he couldn't stand it anymore.

"Fuck me, Johnnie! Stick it in and fuck me hard! Please!"

He didn't have to ask me twice.

He raised his ass to meet my cock, which naturally spread his perfect cheeks. There he was! His beauty knew no limits, and I carefully and pleasantly lubed his ass crack, and the head of my cock, with the KY Jelly we'd gotten on our 7-11 run earlier.

Sander moaned as I massaged his crack with the aromatic lubricant, and I mounted him and slowly started pushing my very stiff cock into his waiting anus. He moaned in great ecstasy, and began slowly moving against me dick until his butt cheeks touched the base of my aroused member. And then I felt his ass grip my cock as he released a pleasured sigh.

"Fuck me, Johnnie. Hard. Fast. Let me feel you!" he passionately declared. "It feels so good! Fucking hell, it feels nice! Ahhhhh...."

My rhythm increased, and he power bottomed at the same time, rising up to meet each thrust with his hips and gorgeous ass.

I rested my hands against his smooth back and started massaging him, which just increased his pleasure. A good half an hour later and I was about to cream, no lie. I was feeling things I had never felt before, and I believe I'm a fairly experienced bloke when it comes to that crazy little thing called love.

But my dick—especially my head—was quivering in ways that were simple breathtaking. And through all of this amazing pleasure I could see the fantastic form of the love of my life lying in his own ecstatic place. This was definitely working. We'd crossed some kind of sexual threshold.

"I'm gonna cum soon, Pokey! I'm gonna cum!"

"Cum inside me! I need to feel you inside me, Johnnie!"

"Yes!" I managed, before what seemed like a liter of ejaculate flew into his hole. There was so much cum that it was already squeezing out as the load was still shooting inside him.

He groaned with pleasure, and pulled himself away. That's when he rolled me onto my

368

back and raised my legs. With missing a beat he mounted my ass, face to face, and fucked me like he meant it.

He felt so good, his perfect uncut cock plowing deep inside me. I could see his beautiful eyes and he breathed heavy breaths, taking me to absolute heaven above.

"I love you so much, Johnnie! Do you like it? Do you feel good?"

"Fucking right I do! Oh, man, it's awesome!" I told him as he drilled my ass with his rock hard dick. I could feel his foreskin moving back and forth against my hole, and I remember how much I loved looking at his strong shoulders as he pushed my legs back so he could go even deeper.

No pain. No bother at all. No movements of a selfish lover. Just mad, hot, passionate anal sex between two men who loved each other more than anyone on earth. He knew what to do, and I was the happy recipient of the best fucking I'd ever had.

"Where shall I cum?!" he blurted.

"Inside! I want to feel you, too! Sander, cum inside me!" I pleaded in ecstasy. "Oh, God, it's so good..."

Then I felt the warmth of Sander Lars Hansen as he filled me with himself. He dropped onto me and pushed out the last couple of spurts even deeper inside, and we were content to lie in each other's arms until one of us had to pee. It was me! Ha!

The next morning we would drive back to the family home and get the last of Sander's things. Then we would begin our lives anew. Looks like the black rain cloud finally decided to go pick on somebody else for awhile.

The loving team of Johnnie Paul Allen and Sander Lars Hansen was back on the block!

Chapter 28

WHAT A YEAR IT HAD BEEN.

Good in many ways, but you also know firsthand
how difficult it's been.

Sander and I rose out of the horrible place we
had found ourselves, and everything between us has
been better than it ever has.

Jannik still holds hard feelings toward his
brother, but he's getting better each day. They're
talking, and more importantly joking again. They'll
be fine. I also make sure to tread carefully around
Jannik's feelings for me that he had so eloquently
expressed in his letter to me.

One exciting thing for him! He met a boy near his age on Facebook of all places and the two of them are getting on famously. I think there might be something there. They're already making plans about visiting one another.

The lad, Will Gabriels, lives in Yorkshire, England, and is very keen to meet Jannik. I think those two might pull something off together (regarding a visit, you pervs!) in the summertime.

We have Thanksgiving fast approaching, and Christmas after that. Thanksgiving is not a holiday in Denmark, but I've imported it for my family and Danish friends. And they love it! So now it's a tradition.

Marge has a steady girlfriend now. They're totally dating, and all indications are a big thumbs up. She deserves all the happiness in the world, and I'm pulling for them.

I received some bad news about Captain Lanning. He died in a massive car accident caused by a drunk driver. The drunk came out of it without a scratch. The captain didn't. That was a wonderful man who had done nothing but serve others his whole life. What an inglorious end for someone I consider a personal hero.

Elena Kuzmich, the mother of Eugeny, would never see her son again. One day he just stopped coming to visit her at the convalescent hospital where she is expected to live out the rest of her life. She keeps a photograph at her bedside, and wonders why he stopped coming. It's like he just disappeared.

Vladimir Putin got the message. He's backed off on his plans for Ukrainian domination, and is having more fun, it seems, blowing up random targets in Syria under the guise of fighting the Islamic State. Have fun, creepy boy.

Palle and Ingrid moved into our old house and we made their rent payments equal to the mortgage and insurance, so they got a great deal that meets their budget, and it turns out that Sander and I are going to be uncles! What a beautiful place for them to start their family, and we don't care if they ever leave. We love that they're there, and we're sure that the house does too. That's a home that needs happiness and love, and with there soon to be little footsteps in the place, I can't think of what could be more happier than that.

And then there's Thom. Wonderful Thom Bleaker. I got a message to him to contact me as soon as he could, and he did. I told him everything that had happened between Sander and me. He understood, but he was sad. He's still our friend, though, and he plans to come to our Thanksgiving do. I really hope he does. And so does Sander.

Another piece of good news arrived by post. We got a letter from the court telling us that we had, as a matter of course, 30 days to cancel our divorce papers. So guess what we did?

THE FIRST SNOWFALL happened last night. It started as Sander and I were driving home from the Hansen home in Odense.

"Look! There's white stuff falling from the sky," Sander said. "I like white stuff!"

"I know you do. Me too. Especially yours."

"We can get all cozy tonight, and light the wood stove, and just be together. Netflix and Chill," Sander smiled. "Without the Netflix," he added, giving my balls a little friendly squeeze.

"Ah, man, you tryin' ta kill me? I just gave you sweet lovin' five minutes ago!" I said in my lousy Isaac Hayes South Park Chef impersonation.

"And you will again. I need a fuck from the tall man with the yellow hair," he informed me.

"Okay."

The drive was especially nice, the aroma of Sander's Blue Stratos cologne filling the car. The yellowish glow of the lights of Copenhagen through the snow began filling the horizon and I reflected on all that had transpired to put me in this place I found so dear.

Had my parents been more understanding and supportive of me would I have ever left home and gone to sea? Absolutely not.

My fantastic grandparents who were and are my familial rock provided the springboard I needed to know that this blond gay kid could set out and accomplish anything he desired in life. And damned if he hadn't gotten it in spades.

In just a couple of years my angelic brother and sister, who all but worship Sander and me, will be over here where they'll, for the first time in their sweet lives, be allowed to untangle themselves from the confusion that are our parents and thrive on their own.

Right now, perhaps walking the streets of Copenhagen, or Odense, or some other university town in this delightful kingdom are the special ones who will become the loves of their lives. I had that thought one time looking down from an airliner window and look what happened to me.

Life is difficult sometimes, and the things we are forced to endure through no fault of our own can be very daunting. But when your support system is the Family Hansen of Odense, Denmark, there's nothing that can't be overcome.

And then I look at the man to my right . . .

"What?" he smiles.

"Nothing," I reply. "Just looking."

"Oh! I can look back too, you know?" he chuckles. "Besides, there's nothing to see here! Go back inside your homes, people! There's nothing to see here!" he jokes.

"Oh, I think there is."

"Cocks don't count!" he says.

"Nope. It's so much more than that," I tell him. "So very much more than that, Pokey."

He acknowledged my observations with a dismissive wave of his hand, and looked out at the passing towns and countryside. "I love you, Johnnie," he said.

"I love you more," I said. And then he said something that touched me in a way that nothing had ever done before.

"You know how much I love Marge, right?" Sander began. "I mean, that she helped you get my brother back, and how she absolutely loves you, Johnnie, and you know she has a heart as big as the moon."

"You'll get no argument from me, Pokes. I owe that woman our lives, and she means more to me than practically anyone I've ever known," I confessed. Then he slowly turned to me and took my hand in his.

> "So, I will say, whatever comes, I'll cherish what we are... I promise that the time we had was never spent in vain...
>
> "Yet one day, or night, or time that's yet to be... Whether sun or breeze or rain-a-pouring, the truth will come, Long before morning.
>
> "We'll conquer the fear that sent us this warning; and this will come, Long before morning."

"Where the fuck did you hear that?" I asked him, betraying complete surprise in my voice. "She made me read it the first week we broke up. The first night, in fact! Pokey, where'd you get it?"

"She drove out to Gelsted and left it on my car. It gave me hope, Johnnie. It really did," he explained. "And one day she took me out to lunch to talk with me about everything. That's when I found it out," he said.

"Found what out?"

"That she wrote it. For us."

My heart burst with so much love for Marge. As if she wasn't already at the top of my list, that just did it.

Heading east, as we were, and feeling a warmth inside that knows no adequate description, we could see the lightening of the eastern sky.

Soon the sun would rise, and morning, finally, would be here.

THE AUTHOR of the *Happy Endings Sleepover* Series is Cade Jay Hathaway. He lives in Denmark with Lasse, the man he continues to love more than life. The two live near Copenhagen where Mr. Hathaway continues his work for the clandestine services of the United States Government.

96036293R00228

Made in the USA
Lexington, KY
15 August 2018